For Mam and Dad,
Thanks for everything.

For those gripped in the darkness of depression,
may you find the light.

ACKNOWLEDGEMENTS

I would like to express my sincere gratitude to Siobhán Parkinson for her expertise in the editing and publishing process and for having faith in my ability to bring Flick to life. Thanks also to Elaina O Neill in Little Island for all the work, which she undertook in such a cheerful yet professional manner.

To Seamus Cashman, a great mentor, thanks so much for all your advice and support. Thanks to my writing group buddies, especially Juliette, Paddy and Patricia, for their helpful feedback. Thanks also to those who reviewed and critiqued the manuscript. I'm grateful to Sine Quinn for all her encouragement.

To my parents, Tom and Betty, and my brothers and sisters. I'm lucky to have grown up in such a great family.

Finally to my darling husband Johnny for believing in me and motivating me and always being there and to my amazing children for their equal measure of inspiration and distraction.

CHAPTER 1

My eyes are closed but I'm awake. I swallow and groan. My head pounds. I gently pull my tongue, dry and rough, from the roof of my mouth. I stink of smoke; it lingers in my nose, my mouth and on last night's clothes – which I'm still wearing. I don't want to breathe or swallow or move. I try to remember how the night ended – the club, the girls, how I got home – but can't. Just don't think, my brain whispers.

I lie there, hearing a thudding in my head, and only realise when Mam's opening the door that it's her, having come up the stairs and knocked. Damn it, I groan inwardly. She comes over and sits on the side of the bed. She nudges me, but I don't respond. I don't have the energy to. She prods me again persistently and I grunt, feigning deep sleep.

'Felicity, how was last night?' she whispers enthusiastically.

I'm going to be sick if I have to talk or think, so I don't say anything.

'That good, eh?' she says, bending to pick some

clothes off the floor. 'I wish you'd put your clothes away when you're finished with them,' she says. 'It's not such a difficult thing to do.'

I groan sleepily and turn my back, hoping she'll get the message. The last bloody thing I need today is a lecture on the state of my room.

'Have you still got your clothes on from last night?' she suddenly asks, pulling the covers back.

Uh-oh, I think. Here we go!

'And you stink of smoke – were you smoking?' I can tell she's looking at me even though my eyes have refused to open. I listen to her breathing, waiting. There's no excuse to give, nothing that will pacify Mam so I stay tight-lipped and hope for the best. Is she going? I wonder after a moment when she, too, has remained silent. Please God may she go and let me die in peace, I silently beg.

'Felicity, wake up,' she says, pulling at the quilt. I reluctantly turn back towards her which, in hindsight, was the beginning of the end.

'Oh my God, what is that on your neck?' she gasps.

My eyes flicker open and my hand instinctively goes to cover whatever's there.

'Jesus, what the hell did you get up to last night?'

'Nothing,' I croak, sitting up on the bed.

It's a bad move, I can feel my stomach beginning to retch. Concentrate, Flick, I warn myself. 'I don't need the Spanish Inquisition every time I've had a night out, Mam,' I begin, 'and I wasn't …' I stop, jump off the bed and race towards the en suite. I get there but of course I don't reach the loo and I puke all over the floor. I can't move another inch so I just bend over and get sick some more. A lot more. Even when there's absolutely nothing left in my stomach I'm still retching. Finally it's over and I feel dizzy from the exertion. Even the blood pulsing through my veins hurts; my head's still pounding and my legs feel like jelly. I have to lie down. I grab a towel and wipe my face as I make my way back to bed. Mam just stands there staring, too much in shock to even ask how I am. I can see the anger on her face but at this moment in time I just don't have the energy to care.

'What the hell were you drinking last night?' she shouts. She waits but I don't reply. 'Or did you take something? Are you on something?' she persists.

'No,' I groan. 'It was probably the burger I ate on the way home,' I try lamely.

'Don't lie to me, Felicity,' she snaps.

'Can we talk later?' I beg.

'Aren't you even going to brush your teeth or clean yourself up?' she asks incredulously as I kick off my boots and skirt and lie on the bed. '*Felicity!*'

Her shout goes through my whole body.

'What the hell is wrong with you? You're a bloody

mess.' She watches as I close my eyes, unable to say anything. She stands for a few moments in silence. I don't hear her leaving.

I wake on and off and stumble out to the loo a few times. It is spotless. I hadn't even heard Mam coming back in and cleaning up. At some stage I think I'll never drink again, but I know that too will pass. My mouth tastes stale, like an ashtray, and I wish I had the energy to brush my teeth but I don't. I sleep some more and don't allow myself to think of the night before, the drink or Tom. Instead I dream endlessly of food and I eventually wake, starving.

The light has gone from the room and I look at my mobile: 21.15. I crawl out of bed and turn on the shower in the bathroom. I just about manage to wash and dry myself before my stomach begins to heave again. All I want to do is lie down and die but I know if I don't get some painkillers and grub it could be a very painful death.

The telly's on in the sitting-room as I tiptoe past into the kitchen and grab as much stuff as I can, as quickly as possible, before heading upstairs again. I'm halfway up when the sitting-room door opens. I freeze. Mam stares up at me, stony-faced before turning and walking across the hall. I head back to my little sanctuary. Tomorrow is going to be awful.

CHAPTER 2

I wake at about six and listen to Dad bustling around before he heads out to work. I wonder what Mam has told him and think of the inevitable showdown that lies ahead. I haul myself up shortly after seven. It's probably the first time Mam hasn't had to roar at me or drag me out of bed since I was four. The moment I move, my head begins to throb again so it takes me ages to get ready. I drag myself into the bathroom and stare at myself in the mirror. Usually I look tanned and healthy but today I look pale and drained, my blue eyes look lifeless and my shoulder-length brown hair is limp and dull. I gather it into a ponytail to tie it up and that's when I see it, this massive lovebite that covers half of the left hand side of my neck. Oh my God, I think, beginning to plaster it in make-up, it really is gross. The make-up doesn't work; instead of hiding it, the orange streak highlights it even more.

'Damn it,' I whisper, pulling at my collar, then at my hair in the hope of covering the incriminating evidence. Nothing works. As a last resort I grab my woolly school scarf and, ignoring the sun streaming in the window, wrap it around my neck. 'Nothing or no one is going to budge you today,' I promise, heading downstairs.

The dread of confronting Mam gets stronger with every step I take. How the hell am I going to explain it and get away alive? I wonder. Life just wouldn't be worth living if I was to ignore or deny what's happened and would definitely prompt counselling in Mam's books. Arguing would be fatal. What I should do is just quietly apologise and then listen as she rants and raves until she has it all out of her system. I look at my watch; it's a quarter to eight, which gives her a good twenty minutes of a lecture before I grovel for forgiveness. She'll sort things out with Dad, explain how she's given me the third degree and a hefty grounding and it will all be forgotten about by the time I get home. Happy days!

When I get to the kitchen door I take a deep breath and turn the handle. I can't believe it: it's cold and empty – no table set, no lunch made for me to take to school, no warm smell of toast or coffee. An empty kitchen was not what I was expecting, and I'm not sure whether to be happy or disappointed – prolonging the ordeal will just make it worse. Waiting for something bad to happen is just as bad as the bloody thing happening.

I grab a bowl of cereal, pour too much milk on it and wonder whether to just go up to her room and apologise or get the hell out while the coast is clear. I'm still thinking when she walks in. I look up and open my mouth to say something but she ignores me completely, grabs her bag and keys from the counter, turns and walks away. Within seconds I hear the front door slam behind her. I sit in shocked silence. Oh my God, I think, she's definitely mad. Even if I came on my hands and knees with a list of counsellors in one hand and a list of AA groups in the other, begging for forgiveness, she'd probably still want to kill me. I'm doomed. With this thought in mind I slowly pick up my bag, lock up and head to school. At least there things won't be any worse …

Fee and Kar catch up with me as I trudge along.

'So, you survived?' Fee says with a grin, her mad red curls falling carelessly around her freckled face.

'For a few more hours anyway,' I say. Then I give them a run-down on my hangover saga with Mam and how the worst is yet to come. Fee's all sympathetic, but Kar just laughs.

'Gee, thanks,' I say, shooting her a look that could kill.

Kar is gorgeous-looking, like she could be a model; I swear, she's got the perfect figure, beautiful blonde hair and the brightest, bluest eyes I've ever seen. Sometimes it's hard to stop looking at her. What's even cooler is that she doesn't give a damn about anything, ever, so she does the maddest things.

'It's just your Mam's so proper and perfect. I would

love to have been there to see the look on her face.'
Kar's still grinning like mad.

'It wasn't pretty,' I say.

'So, you and Tom must have had a good time,' she continues.

'I can't really remember that much,' I admit, not wanting to think about it. The only thing I do remember was pretending that I was going to be sick all over him when he dragged me outside and started getting all romantic and heavy. It was pathetic, really, but it worked. He reluctantly followed me back inside and watched while I got drunker and drunker.

'So, are you two going out together?' Fee asks.

'No,' I snort in disgust.

'But he's gorgeous,' she sighs.

'He's an idiot,' I snap.

'When are we ever going to find a guy that you actually like and want to go out with?' Kar asks with a small smirk.

'Well, we certainly won't find him in this dump,' I say nodding towards the school ahead, trying not to go red.

The taunting continues all day, from both the girls and the guys. Science class is the worst – I absolutely HATE science, not just because I haven't a clue of ninety-nine per cent of the stuff but also because Cunningham, our science teacher, is a real dragon and she hates me, I swear she does. Today she's talking about the male reproductive system of all bloody things. Almost immediately the jeers begin; people are nudging and poking me and some of the lads start throwing stuff at me and instead of Cunningham dealing with anyone else she just gets me to read. I'm *mortified*. And right in the middle of all that, Trev, one of Tom's friends who happens to be sitting behind us, starts pulling at my scarf. He practically strangles me in the process of getting it off me and Cunningham, aka Crabface, looks up and gives out to me for 'not being able to read plain English.'

'Can you please get my scarf back?' I ask Kar after class. The lads are racing by with wolf whistles and smart-assed remarks.

'Hey, Trev,' she roars, 'give us that scarf.'

He laughs and races on, ignoring her.

'Just forget about it,' says Kar. 'People won't even look at it after a few hours. A day or two, tops,' she says.

'Well, that's just great, then.'

'How about pulling your collar up?' Fee suggests.

'That's too noticeable,' I say.

'Right, and a big grey scarf around your neck on a day like today isn't?' asks Kar.

'It's January,' I argue.

'Yeah but, hello, the heat's on, it's boiling in here.'

I turn and stick out my tongue and before I know what's happening she's pushing me against the wall.

'Don't move,' she orders as she fixes my collar.

Don't go red, don't go red, I think but I can feel myself hot all over. I stand rigidly and try to look anywhere but at her.

'Perfect,' she says after a moment. Then she turns and walks on. I follow slowly behind, stuck for words, my heart racing.

'Hey,' comes a voice from behind me.

Every muscle in my body tenses and even before I turn round I know it's him.

'Oh, um, hi, Tom,' I say, going red all over again.

'Hey,' he says with a grin. 'That was good fun the other night.'

'Yeah … yeah it was,' I lie.

'We had some session,' he says with a laugh. 'We'll have to do it again!'

'Yeah,' I agree.

'Maybe next weekend?' he suggests.

'Em, I don't think I'll be out,' I say.

'Well, maybe the weekend after?' he persists.

'Em … I guess … sure,' I agree half-heartedly.

'Great, it's a date,' he smiles.

As he walks away I give a weak grin and wonder how the hell I'm going to get out of this one.

CHAPTER 3

The day doesn't really get any better and even when I reach home I know the worst has yet to come. I'm up in my room trying to distract myself on my guitar when I hear Mam come in the hall door. OK, I think, just get this over and done with. I make my way slowly downstairs, still without a plan. All I know is that I've to get in, apologise and get out, unscarred, as quickly as possible. The only way to do that is to say nothing other than sorry and to agree with absolutely everything she says. I stand outside the door for a few seconds, psyching myself up before heading in.

'Hi,' I say quietly to her back. She doesn't even turn around. I cross my fingers, take a deep breath and dive in. 'I'm sorry, Mam,' I croak, my voice already cracking under the pressure. I clear my throat, 'I was a disgrace at the weekend. I'm really sorry; it won't happen again.'

She spins around. 'Damn right it won't; you're sixteen years old, Felicity, and you're out drinking yourself into oblivion. I've never seen anyone in as bad a state as you were. I just couldn't believe it; I still can't get my head around it. What the hell were you drinking? Where did you even get drink from anyway? Do you know you could have poisoned yourself with that stuff? How the hell am I ever going to trust you again?' She stops and stares at me.

Oh God, she wants me to answer her and I haven't a clue what to say.

'Well, what were you drinking?' she shouts again.

'I wasn't,' I mumble and she automatically clenches her jaw. 'We stopped in Luigi's on the way home and I got a cheeseburger, and it was about half an hour after that when I was home in bed that I began to feel sick.'

'Felicity, don't you dare lie to me,' she says, 'you were totally out of it, so I know for a fact it wasn't the food.'

'I swear, Mam, I'm not.' I stare at her, knowing she's not buying it. I'm desperate now. 'Kar said that she remembers seeing someone near our drinks and she thinks he might have put something in my Coke but he just disappeared when she went back over to the table. She says that's happened there before,' I suddenly blurt out.

Mam's anger turns to shock and for a second I'm relieved.

'Oh my God, did you see anyone? Did your drink taste different?'

I shake my head.

'Who else has it happened to?' Mam asks.

'Kar couldn't remember the girl's name,' I say. 'It

happened a good while ago and I don't think she went to our school. It might even have been just a story.'

'Ring Karen and let me talk to her; she may have a description of that guy.'

I gulp. Then I go to the phone and pretend to ring her number. 'It's ringing out,' I say. 'She had to go to the dentist anyway, but she said she couldn't remember what he looked like, other than that he was tall with brown hair.'

'Don't they have security cameras in those places? I bet they could go back over the tapes – they'd have a better description of the guy. That boy you were with, who was he?' she asks. 'Was he someone you know?'

'Not really,' I murmur.

'He either was or he wasn't, Felicity,' she snaps.

'No,' I gulp, hoping I'm giving the right answer.

'Was he older? Could he have spiked your drink so you'd be with him?'

Uh oh. I wish I'd kept my big mouth shut.

'I think Jen knew him,' I blurt out. 'I don't think it was him and I don't think anyone really spiked my drink; it was the food.'

'I'm ringing the Cove,' she says, ignoring me. 'I'm going to find out about those cameras. And aren't they supposed to have bouncers walking around?'

Crap! 'Mam, it's always packed; they can't check everything.'

'Well, I'm ringing anyway. If they're aware of the

problem they'll be better able to deal with it. When I think what could have happened to you … I'm going to ring the guards as well.'

'Mam, I really think that was just a story about that other girl … and no one else saw anyone near our table. You know Kar – she's always joking around; she probably didn't see anyone either … Seriously, I think it was the food.'

Mam shakes her head. 'It wasn't food poisoning, you were too spaced out.' She pauses. 'And you definitely weren't drinking?'

I gulp and shake my head, unable to speak. 'And you didn't take any drugs?'

'Of course not,' I croak.

She reaches for the phone. 'And Karen definitely doesn't know that girl that was drugged before?' she asks as she dials the number for directory enquiries.

I shake my head again, 'It was just a story going around school,' I murmur. Ohmygod, ohmygod, I'm screwed; she's getting the bloody cops involved. There's still no way I'm telling the truth, though, not now, no way. So I stand watching her as she rings the Cove. Thankfully it rings out. She leaves a message, of course, with her name and number and then she dials the number of the police station. I listen as she retells the story; she's more definite that my drink was spiked with every passing minute. I cringe listening to her and nearly have heart failure when she gives both our names and the phone number. Eventually she hangs up.

'What? What did they say?' I ask.

'They say that without a positive blood sample there's nothing they can do. Neither are there any witnesses to anyone spiking your drink and they have no previous reports regarding something like this ever happening in the club. So they're going to do absolutely nothing.' I sigh with relief.

She's ranting on about how bad the whole system is.

'It doesn't matter, Mam,' I say.

'Of course it does,' she says, staring at me. 'Don't you remember how bad you were? And look at your neck; it's disgraceful.'

My hand automatically covers it. She goes to the cupboard and grabs the Arnica cream, telling me to put some on. 'Didn't you know what he was doing?' she asks. I bite my lip. I can hear the anger back in her voice.

'We were just kissing,' I mumble.

'You have to have respect for yourself, Felicity; you can't let boys just take advantage and do whatever they want.'

'I know,' I say, feeling the first tears sting my eyes. 'I hate myself as much as you do, Mam; I hate that I let this happen,' I blurt and I begin to cry.

'Felicity, of course I don't hate you,' she says quietly after a few seconds, 'and I don't want you to hate yourself.

I'm just worried about what's happened and I'm really scared that it could happen again,' she murmurs.

'It won't happen again.'

'Look, we all make mistakes. I just don't want you making mistakes that might get you into trouble … with boys.'

I look at her and nod before staring again at the floor. She gives me a quick hug.

'Now go back upstairs and try and get your home-work done before dinner,' she says as she pulls away, 'and I'll call you when it's ready.'

I reach the door. 'Thanks, Mam,' I say, relieved that it's all over.

CHAPTER 4

By Friday afternoon I'm totally worn out. All week I've been on my best behaviour at home and have tried to be as invisible as possible in school and it's bloody tough going. The lads were such idiots and never left me alone and as for Mam, she persisted in ringing the Cove every day until someone answered her call. She wasn't impressed when they told her that kids make up stories like that all the time when they want to get themselves off the hook for something. They insisted that no one spiked my drink because things like that don't happen there, nor could I have taken any drink or drugs as they don't serve alcoholic drink in an under-eighteens club and absolutely no drugs are allowed on the premises. Whatever happened to me, they said, happened after I left the Cove and has nothing to do with them. Mam's absolutely disgusted with their attitude and hasn't stopped going on about it since.

So the second I get home I grab some snacks and head straight up to my room to veg out. Mam and Dad got me this really cool laptop at Christmas to help me …

uh ... study. But so far I just tweet and live on Facebook and that's what I'm doing when I hear a noise down-stairs.

What the hell? I jolt upright, then freeze. Someone's trying to get in. The hairs prickle the back of my neck and my stomach flips. No one's supposed to be here; Mam and Dad won't be home for hours. Within sec-onds the door opens and I hear Kev laughing as he bangs it closed behind him, then muffled voices. The other voice sounds extraordinarily like a girl. Seconds later there are pounding footsteps on the stairs before they veer towards Kev's room on the other side of the hall. The talking and laughing stops as bed springs creak. Gross, I think, sliding off the bed.

I sneak downstairs. I open the front door ever so quietly then close it with a bang. I head in and slump onto the couch and switch on the box. I wait. Sure enough, within seconds Kev is thumping down the stairs. I twist towards the door, ready to feign shock at seeing him.

'Hey sis.' He grins as he strolls in.

I'm just about to reply when this tall, thin girl with short blonde hair and beautiful green eyes appears be-hind him. I open my mouth but nothing comes out so I just end up staring.

'Flick this is Becks,' he says.

'Hey,' she says and grins.

'Hiya,' I say, grinning stupidly back and staring at her dumbfoundedly.

* * *

Mam is so not taken with Becks and is even more disgusted when she doesn't like the fab meal Mam's spent the evening preparing.

'I mean, how could anyone not like melon?' Mam asks, looking from one of us to the other when Becks has escaped outside for a cigarette. 'It's practically flavoured water, for God's sake.'

It turns out that she pretty much doesn't like *any* of Mam's dinner; instead she heads out for another ciggy with Kev hot on her heels.

'Go and call them,' Mam orders when the dessert is ready.

I reluctantly do as I'm told and roar for Kev.

'Oh for God's sake, Felicity,' Mam complains, 'I asked you to call Kev and Rebecca, not the whole neighbourhood.'

Mam silently fumes for the rest of the meal; I sit dreaming and Becks doesn't seem too bothered by any of us so that, unfortunately, leaves Kev telling Dad about some football quarter-final he has in three weeks. Dad's gutted that it's the same weekend as the romantic break he's planned with Mam. He looks towards her, his mouth open, ready to suggest something but he closes it again when he sees her stony face. After dinner Kev and Becks spend most of their time out in the freezing cold, smoking, while we chill out in the sitting-room. Mam actually seems to be relaxing a little – that is, until Kev pops his head in at about ten.

'We're wrecked,' he yawns, 'so we're going to hit the hay.'

'OK.' Mam smiles and turns to me. 'Felicity, I didn't realise Rebecca was coming home with Kev and I just put fresh sheets on his bed; can you run up and get some for yours as well? They're in the hot press.'

'Mam,' Kev interrupts, 'Becks can stay in my room.'

'No, she can't,' Mam says, 'she's staying in Felicity's room.'

'Where in my room?' I interrupt.

Mam glares at me. 'In your bed, with you, obviously, or would you have her sleep on the floor?'

'Mam, I'm eighteen,' Kev snaps as he opens the door wider, 'and so is Becks. What's the problem?'

'The problem,' Mam replies adamantly, 'is that this is *our* house and *we* make the rules.' She looks at Dad, then back at Kev. 'And I don't care whether you are eighteen or not; while you're single and under our roof, you'll do as we say.' There's a moment of silence and in it I hear the back door click closed. No doubt Becks is having another cigarette.

'We sleep together all the time in college; what's the difference with sleeping here?' he persists.

'Kevin, I can't do anything about what you do in college; I just hope that you take proper precautions, look after yourself and respect Rebecca,' Mam says, 'but I do have a say in what you do here and I don't think that asking you to sleep in separate rooms for a night or two is too difficult. Now please calm down.'

'You're living in the dark ages,' he growls. 'What the hell is wrong with you?'

'Don't talk like that to your mother,' Dad interrupts in a voice of steel; 'I won't have it.'

'I don't know why I even bothered coming home,' he continues.

'Kevin,' Dad says, 'you keep telling us that you're eighteen so why don't you start acting like it?'

'Well, stop treating me like a little boy,' he snarls.

'You're not sleeping with your girlfriend under our roof and that's final,' Mam says obstinately. Kev gives both Mam and Dad a look of disgust before turning and walking out. I make a quick escape behind him.

I've just made the bed and shoved the last of my clothes into the wardrobe when I hear a noise behind me.

'Love the decor,' Becks smirks as she comes in.

'It's a bit childish really,' I mumble, mortified. The walls and the curtains are pink. 'I should have fixed it up years ago ... I just never bothered.'

I head towards the dressing table and begin to open drawers and rummage for God knows what. Meanwhile Rebecca has dropped her bag and is heading straight for the window.

'Mind if I smoke?' she asks, pulling a joint from her pocket. 'I'll sit here by the window,' she promises as she pushes it open then searches for her lighter.

'No, that's fine,' I lie. 'Maybe I'll just turn off the light, nosy neighbours and all that,' I murmur as I close the door and switch it off.

'Whatever,' she shrugs, taking a long drag. I watch the spark flicker. She inhales deeply, then slowly exhales. How does she make everything look so sexy? I wonder. I don't realise I'm staring at her till she looks over and offers me a drag.

'Thanks,' I say, walking over and taking it. Almost immediately I feel my head go light; after the second drag it starts to spin. 'Wow, that's good stuff,' I say.

'The best,' she says. We drift in and out of conversations; she never stops complaining about her father while saying how cool and sexy and gorgeous Dad is. I laugh embarrassedly again.

'This stuff is definitely going to my head,' I admit after a little while.

'Hey, have you ever had a blow-back?' she asks.

'I've never even heard of it,' I say with a yawn.

'Well, I'd have one end of the joint in my mouth and

you'd have the lit end in yours and I'd just blow it into your mouth.'

'What? There's no way I'm doing that.'

She laughs. 'Well, I suppose we can do it without the joint. Here, I'll show you.' She inhales on the end of the joint then leans towards me until her lips are on mine and she's gently blowing smoke into my mouth. I pull away in shock. Within milliseconds all my senses are on edge and I'm wide awake. She looks at me, still grinning, and I immediately wish I hadn't reacted the way I did.

'Wow, I wasn't ready for that,' I babble. 'What do you call it again?'

'A blow-back.' She sniffs as she stares into the empty garden below. She takes another drag then hands it to me. I take a few puffs and get all giddy and brave.

'Hey, do you mind if we try that blow-back thing again?' I ask. I gulp back the fear that's causing a lump in my throat.

'Sure,' she shrugs. She takes a long drag and leans towards me again, I slowly part my lips and close my eyes. Gently her mouth presses on mine, I inhale deeply. Please may this last for ever, I pray, but already I feel her pulling away. In desperation I lean towards her and I press my lips ever so slightly against her. She kisses me back and a shiver runs down my spine. Thank you, God, I think. Her kiss is soft and I never want it to end but all too soon she's pulling away again. I stare at her, not understanding why the kiss has ended, but wait, still hopeful.

'I want to smoke the end of this before it burns out,' she explains.

'Sure,' I nod, watching her. Eventually she flicks the stub out the window. I make a mental note to find it in the morning before we have another inquisition. When I look back towards her she's staring at me. I give a small smile as she leans towards me, then she hesitates.

'So you're not worried about your nosy neighbours?' she whispers. I can't even speak, just shake my head. She smirks just before her lips touch mine, and I'm in heaven again and oh my God she's so sweet and gorgeous and I'm just melting. After a few minutes she pulls away again. 'I'm wrecked, I have to go to bed,' she says, standing up.

'Oh yeah, me too,' I say, trying to sound cool and relaxed. She turns and heads towards the en suite and I'm left sitting alone with my pounding heart in the darkness.

CHAPTER 5

I spend so long in the bathroom fixing myself up and imagining what's going to happen and what I'm supposed to do that when I come out Becks is in a deep sleep – she's even snoring. I make as much noise as I can getting into bed and even have a mild coughing fit in the hope of waking her but nothing works. I stay awake most of the night in the hope that she'll remember me and wake up but she doesn't budge. At about five I give up and my eyes finally close. There's always tomorrow, I think as I nod off. But by the time I wake up Becks has gone. I throw on my dressing-gown and race downstairs to find Mam sitting at the table alone.

'Where's Becks? And Kev?' I pant.

'Oh, good morning, hon. How are you? Did you sleep well?'

'Yeah, yeah, so where are the others?'

'Well, your Dad's golfing and Kevin and Rebecca have gone out,' she says.

'Out? Out where?' I ask, hoping they're just out smoking again.

'You know Kev,' Mam says, 'he never tells me anything.' She goes back to reading her paper while I trudge back upstairs. Although I shower and dress I spend the rest of the morning lying on my bed, totally depressed. I wake to the sound of the front door slamming.

'Kev-in,' Mam wails, 'do you have to be so aggressive?'

There's no response, just footsteps on the stairs.

'Hurry, Becks,' Kev pleads as he heads towards his room, 'I don't want us to be late.' Suddenly Becks breezes in. I stare at her. She's red-faced and red-nosed from the cold and looking prettier than ever.

'Hi,' she says.

'Hey,' I reply as coolly as I can.

She grabs her bag and pulls out leggings and a top; she's stripped and changed in seconds. Then she bends and begins to pack up the rest of her things.

'What's the story?' I ask in what I hope is an 'I don't care' voice.

'There's some mystery tour for Dave's birthday; we all have to be on the bus at two, before he gets there.'

'Right,' I reply, 'but why are you taking your bags?'

She grins. 'Kev was really peeved that he had to sleep alone last night so one of the lads is putting us up tonight.'

'Does Mam –'

'Becks, come on, we'll be late,' Kev roars as he races downstairs.

'Ah, relax,' she says as she continues to stuff creams

into her bag. She zips it up and walks towards the bathroom where she starts putting on make-up. I follow her and lean against the door.

'That should be good,' I lie. She shrugs while grabbing the rest of her stuff, turns and nearly bumps into me. 'Oh, sorry,' I say, moving out of the way.

'Come on, Rebecca,' Kev shouts. She picks up her case and rolls it towards the door, I follow. I hear Dad and Kev's voices in the hall. 'Becks,' he shouts again.

'Coming,' she calls, then stops and turns back to me. 'I absolutely hate when people shout at me; it's so bloody rude,' she says. I nod stupidly in agreement. She looks at me, then, letting go of her case, she bends towards me and kisses me right then and there on the mouth. I'm shocked and thrilled all at once but then I hear Kev charging back up the stairs. I begin to pull away but Rebecca continues to kiss me. Oh my God, we're going to get caught, my brain screams as every muscle in my body goes rigid. At the last possible second she stops, turns and puts her hand on her bag, just as Kev appears.

'I was about to call you,' she says calmly. 'Will you carry this down?' He grabs the case and looks towards me, then looks again.

'What's up with you?' he asks seeing my red face and shocked expression.

'Nothing,' I say turning away.

'Becks, we'll be late,' he says.

'Kev, it's half past one and it takes fifteen minutes to get to the bus that leaves at two; you do the math. I need to pee.' She turns and walks towards the bathroom.

'There'll be traffic,' he shouts as she closes the door, 'and we want to be there *before* two, not *at* two.' There's no response from Becks. I raise my eyebrows and smirk.

'Don't say a word,' he grunts as I open my mouth to speak.

'I was just going to say goodbye.'

'Whatever,' he says and heads out the door. 'Just hurry,' he shouts back to the closed door, 'I'll be in the car with Dad.' He thumps back down the stairs and I wait for Rebecca. Within a minute she's back.

'Now, where were we?' she asks. I feel like a puppy dog waiting for a treat and ready to do anything to get it. She pushes me gently towards the wall and begins kissing me again. I can hear the car starting downstairs and I try not to think of Kev and Dad waiting. She'll be gone in a minute – just enjoy it, I think. The horn blows but she ignores it. She must really, really like me, I think; she doesn't even want to go! Abruptly she pulls away and gives a quick grin before turning and striding towards the bathroom. She looks in the mirror, puts on more lippy, fixes her hair and heads out the door.

'Thanks,' I say lamely, following her downstairs. She just smiles. I want to ask her when I'll see her again and how we'll organise it. I want to discuss where we could meet and what we'd do, but I don't. She has her hand on the door and I'm standing so close to her and silently praying that she'll kiss me again when Mam appears out of nowhere. I take a step back and automatically turn puce.

'Oh,' she says, 'I thought you had gone ages ago.'

Rebecca gives me a dazzling smile before opening the door. 'See ye,' she calls over her shoulder as she walks away.

'I can't believe she didn't even say thank you,' Mam whispers before heading back into the kitchen.

I stand in the porch watching her go. 'I might see you sometime around college; I'm coming up to see Kev at some stage,' I call. Go on, Flick, tell the whole world, I think as our neighbour looks up from his gardening. Becks doesn't reply, just opens the car door and slides into the back seat wordlessly. I wave as they speed off. No one waves back.

CHAPTER 6

I dare not ask Mam if I can go out with the girls this weekend and instead spend all my time up in my room practising one of my favourite Snow Patrol songs, 'Chasing Cars', on the guitar, and dreaming of Becks.

'Oh my God, I really love that song,' Fee says on Monday morning when she hears me singing it.

'I know; it's so cool. I'm nearly able to play it.'

'Wow,' she breathes. Of course she's not so impressed when I tell her that Kev was home at the weekend, and I don't dare mention Rebecca.

'What?' she screams. 'You're kidding me?'

'Look, I'm sorry, Fee. I swear I didn't know he was coming and he was gone first thing the next morning.'

'Jeez, Flick, you could have at least texted and pretended you needed a book or something and I could have brought it up! I can't believe you never even thought of me.'

I bite my lip. 'Sorry, Fee.'

She's still going on about it on Tuesday. All the while I've been thinking of a way to see Becks again. On

Wednesday I stop putting things off and ring Kev. He's in foul humour.

'So, how's Becks?' I ask after a few minutes.

'She's gone,' he says matter of factly, 'and I don't give a damn how she is.'

'Gone? Gone where?' I'm horrified.

'We've split,' he says grudgingly.

'Oh my God, really?' I ask.

He doesn't reply. My mind is racing. This is definitely a sign, I think.

'Look, I have to go,' Kev says.

'Wait,' I say, 'I wanted to ask you something.' It takes a while but after a lot of persuading I manage to coax him into letting me, Fee and Kar come and stay with him the weekend of his match. I figure it's the best weekend, what with Mam and Dad being away, and I'm hoping that once the girls get a few drinks into them and Kev starts having his beloved match analysis I'll be able to sneak off to look for Rebecca. How I'm going to find her is another matter, but I'll think about that later.

I'm all excited when I meet Kar and Fee on the way to school on Thursday morning.

'OK, spill the beans, Costello, what is it?' Kar says.

'Let me guess,' Fee interrupts, 'Tom wants you to go steady?'

'No,' I snort in disgust.

Kar laughs.

'I was talking to Kev last night,' I begin.

'And you're getting excited about that?' Kar asks, turning her nose up. 'You're just weird, Costello!'

'Oh my God, what did he say? You do know your brother is the finest guy in this damn town?' Fee says.

'Except he's not in this town,' Kar interrupts.

'Don't I know it,' she says.

Fee and Kev have kissed on at least two occasions, which has certainly not put Fee off liking him, crazy as that seemed to me. 'He kept going on about this big football match that he has in two weeks,' I say.

'Bloody football,' Fee butts in. 'I mean, what the hell do guys see in running after a damn ball around a field?'

'It's all about skill and it's not only guys that do it,' I say.

'Well, it drives me crazy. I can't stand the bloody game!'

'That's a pity,' I say, 'because he did say he'd love if we went up to see it.'

'What?' she screams.

'He said if we wanted to go and see the match, we could, and we could kip in his house that night! But I'll tell him you're not interested.'

'Oh, shut up!' she says. 'You know I'd pretend to be interested in sumo wrestling if Kev was involved.'

I laugh. 'What about you, Kar?'

'Excluding your dear brother,' says Kar, 'there will be twenty-nine eligible players, a ref, two sideline officials, coaches and a college bar full of potentials, so yeah, of course I'm there! And you never know, Costello, you might even get lucky!'

'You know what? I think I just might.'

The next two weeks are just mad. We discuss and plan our weekend away over and over again and then it's Friday and Mam and Dad are dropping me to Kar's house. Already I have butterflies in my stomach.

We spend Friday night in Kar's bedroom listening to CDs, eating pizza, trying on outfits, painting nails, putting on fake tans and listening to Kar telling Fee how to hook Kev. Most of it involves Fee not looking at or talking to Kev at all.

'So you're sure your Mam will let us go tomorrow?' I ask as we finally drag ourselves into bed.

'For the tenth time, yes,' Kar says. 'You know I can twist Mom round my little finger so stop going on about it.'

'OK, OK, I'm just making sure.'

In the morning I wake to Kings of Leon blasting out of Kar's stereo and immediately cover my head with my pillow.

'Wakey wakey, sleepy head,' Kar shouts, jumping up and down on the bed.

'I love this song,' Fee squeals and follows suit.

'Can't you at least turn it down? It's hurting my head,' I complain. The bouncing stops and I'm just sighing with relief when the covers are ripped off me and Kar pushes me out of bed. I land with a thud.

'Ow, I bloody well –'

The girls are on top of me, tickling me before I get the chance to say any more. I squeal and try to push them off but they won't give up. I'm half laughing, half screaming when the door opens. Both Kar and Fee look towards it but it's impossible for me to see who's there.

'What the hell are youse screaming at, you bunch of lezzers?' barks Ryan, Kar's brother.

'Get the hell out of my room,' Kar shouts, grabbing a shoe and throwing it at him.

'Lesbos,' he sneers as he ducks for cover. Fee throws another one and, seeing my opportunity, I wriggle free and stand up. 'Oh, a threesome!'

I turn puce while Kar flings a hairbrush. 'You're such a sleaze, Ryan,' she shouts, missing him yet again. He starts making kissing noises.

'Mom,' Kar calls, 'Ryan won't get out of my room.'

'*Mom*,' he mimics.

I don't realise I've done it till Kar's sandal is whirling through the air. It hits Ryan on the ear. Both Kar and Fee gasp. I just stand stupidly with my mouth open. He touches his ear in disbelief before striding towards me with this weird smirk on his face. I begin to back away and almost immediately fall over Kar's other sandal. Ryan pounces the moment I hit the ground, pinning my hands above my head. I don't know whether to laugh or cry. I look up into his face as his piercing blue eyes stare down at me.

He grins. 'Lucky shot Costello.'

I swallow.

The girls spring to my rescue. Kar dives on Ryan's back, making him fall right on top of me, while Fee, as always, follows. For those seconds Ryan's head is right by mine, his lips against my ear.

'Hey,' he whispers, 'at last we're finally getting to know one another.'

'I can't breathe,' I whisper back.

'Get off,' he roars at Kar and Fee; 'you're hurting her.' He throws them off his back in one move and drags me to my feet. He gives my hand the smallest squeeze and stares at me for a second or two more. 'Are you OK?'

I nod. 'I'm sorry,' I say hoarsely.

'Are you crazy?' Kar shrieks. 'What the hell are you apologising to him for?'

'Don't be; I'm not,' he whispers as Kar continues to shriek. Then he turns and walks away. I catch Fee staring at me, her eyebrows raised quizzically while Kar tells Ryan to go to hell and slams the door after him. I shake my head adamantly, silently warning Fee to keep quiet, and quickly disappear into the bathroom.

* * *

The traffic is crap and it doesn't help that Kar's Mam takes a wrong turn on the way to the bus stop.

'Mom, what the hell are you doing?' Kar shouts.

We're stuck behind a truck on a one-way street.

'Isn't this the way?' her Mam asks innocently.

'It's the other direction.'

I begin to laugh, not at what Kar has just said, but with relief. We've missed the bus; we can't go! All night I've had the worst dreams of things going horribly wrong with Fee and Kev and of searching for Becks and never finding her or finding her and the others finding us! Now I can relax knowing none of that can happen and I won't have to lie to Mam and Dad either. Kar looks at me, then at Fee, then back to me.

'I don't believe this,' she says, 'you're laughing, she's crying! Am I the only sane person in this car?' She doesn't wait for the answer. 'Look, Mom, just take us to the train station.'

The smile fades from my face. 'But ... but ... I can't afford the train,' I say lamely.

'It's OK,' Kar says, 'Mom'll pay; it's her fault we've missed the bus.'

Half an hour later we're sitting on the train, and as we make our way out of the station I bury my niggling doubts and join in the girls' excited chatter. It's going to be a great weekend!

CHAPTER 8

In the end we only get to see about twenty minutes of Kev's match, which suits us just fine. When it's over Kar insists we get some grub, and for the umpteenth time goes over how we're supposed to act when we get to the pub and the bouncers. Finally it's time to head back.

Fee actually begins to jog just to get there quicker which I've never seen her do before. Mind you, it lasts for all of ten seconds before she slows to a fast walk.

'For God's sake,' Kar snaps, 'act cool.'

We queue up, fake IDs ready, but all it takes is for Kar to bat her eyelids and pout her lips for us to get in. She struts through the crowd so confidently that I can see people stopping and staring. When she nears the bar she turns and waits for us.

'OK,' she hisses, 'I see them; two o' clock but don't look now.'

'Oh for God's sake, Kar,' I say, 'he's my brother. Where the hell is he?'

'There,' Fee gasps, pointing, before Kar has time to answer.

'Ohmygod, please tell me he hasn't seen you *pointing*

at him and would you take that silly look off your face, Fee,' Kar orders, 'or he'll run a bloody mile.'

I walk over to Kev, leaving Fee and Kar to follow behind.

'Hey, sis.' He smiles, tousling my hair.

'Ke-ev,' I groan, trying to put my hair right, just as Fee and Kar come up to us.

'Hey, how's it going?' Kev is all smiles.

'*Hey.*' Fee is beaming all over her face.

Kar sighs and gives a quick hi.

'So, great win –' I begin.

'Girls, this is Mike,' Kev interrupts as some guy hands him a pint. 'You might have seen his lovely legs on the field.'

Mike pulls his jeans up slightly and wiggles his leg.

'Mike is my housemate,' says Kev, 'not by choice, of course.'

'Shut up Kev,' Mike interrupts, 'on to more important matters.' He edges in closer. 'What will the lovely ladies have to drink?'

'So, is he single?' Fee asks Kev as Mike heads back to the bar.

'It depends on who wants to know.' Kev smirks.

'No, it's not for me; I was just wondering for Flick and Kar,' she stutters.

'Oh, right, why, are you going out with some one?' he asks.

'Ah no, not at all,' she gushes, turning an even deeper red.

'So you're not interested in Mike?' Kev persists.

'No,' Fee gulps.

'How come?' he asks innocently.

'I … I,' she looks quickly towards Kar, knowing she has already said too much. 'He's just not my type,' she replies quickly.

'And what is your type?' he asks, raising an eyebrow.

Fee gazes at him with this lovesick look on her face.

'Great; just great,' Kar hisses sarcastically beside me. 'So much for staying cool.'

'Shut up Kev,' I interrupt.

Kev gives Fee a last quick look before turning to me. 'He's single – nobody's willing to take him so he's as free as a bird!' he says.

I feel Kar nudge me. 'Game on!' she whispers.

Mike arrives back from the bar. 'For the lovely ladies,' he says, handing us our drinks.

Almost immediately someone comes over to congratulate them and Fee is back in front of us.

'Well done with Kev! Really well played!' Kar says sarcastically.

'It wasn't my fault. He backed me into a corner,' Fee replies. 'Anyway, what do you think of Mike?'

'He's got potential,' Kar says.

'Yeah, he's cute,' I reply.

He's certainly good looking, for a bloke. He's a little taller than Kev with dark curly hair that's gone a little shaggy and he's really fit looking.

As if sensing that he's being scrutinised, Mike looks over and flashes a quick smile. I smile back. Aghhh, I think, looking quickly away.

'I saw that,' Kar interrupts, 'a very sly tactic, playing the Ms Sweet and Shy card. This is going to make for a very interesting night.' She immediately turns and heads back towards the lads.

'I thought one of the rules was to play it cool if you were interested in someone,' Fee growls as she stares after Kar who's now laughing with them.

'You know Kar,' I say, 'she makes up her own as she goes along. But hey, I'm just heading to the loo, why don't you go over to Kev?'

'Really?' she asks.

'Defo,' I say, 'I know if I was interested in someone I wouldn't be waiting till the end of the night to make a move … Life's too short, Fee.'

'You're right,' she says delightedly. I turn and within seconds I'm lost in the crowd. I give a final look back; all four are chatting away. OK, I think, now all I have to do is find her! I just hope she's here somewhere.

CHAPTER 9

The bar is mobbed and I begin to wonder whether there's any point in looking for her and what I'd even say if I did find her. I turn abruptly to head back to the others and collide with some girl.

'Jeez, I'm really sorry,' I begin.

She gasps and quickly wipes her alcohol-soaked top.

'Can't you bloody well watch where you're going?' she snaps.

I bite my lip. 'Sorry,' I mumble again but she's storming away. I look after her, feeling embarrassed, and am just about to turn back when someone catches my eye. I look again and there's Rebecca laughing and talking and looking as beautiful as ever. I stand frozen and wonder again if I should just walk away and live with my dreams and memories. *Life's too short*, I hear my voice telling Fee. And you know she likes you. Go on – it'll be worth it in the end!

I squeeze through the crowd, veering towards the bar so that I come up behind her, then quietly call her name in the hope that everyone else will continue on with their conversation.

'Hi Becks,' I say to her back.

She doesn't respond. Some of the gang around her stop talking and peer over at me. I ignore the girls, tap her on the back and call her name again. She turns and for a second an uncertain look crosses her face.

'It's Flick … Kev's sister,' I falter. 'How are you?'

'Oh my God, Flick,' she says with a laugh, 'what are you doing here?'

'I, uh … I was up watching Kev's match and then we came drinking,' I reply with a smile. 'So, how are things?' I ask.

'Great,' she says, taking a sip of her cocktail; 'better than ever.' She gives a knowing look towards her friends. 'Hey, guys, did I tell ye about going down to Kev's home for the weekend?'

And I stand there and stupidly listen while she drools over how gorgeous Dad was and scoffs at Kev for being a real mammy's boy and Mam for being Mam.

'You don't half like the older men, Becks,' someone says and there's another roar of laughter.

She turns back towards me with a smirk. 'So –' she begins just as her phone starts to ring. This is all an act, just so the others won't know, I think, looking into her face. She beams at me as she says a quick goodbye to whoever it is on the other end and I swear my heart skips a beat. I smile at her but she ignores me and turns back towards the girls with a squeal of delight.

'You'll never guess!' she screeches.

'What? Tell us,' they laugh, squeezing in closer around her. I stand watching their backs for a few seconds longer. Becks has already forgotten about me. With a sigh I walk slowly away.

It doesn't take me long to get back to the others. Kev and Fee are now as close to one another as is humanly possible without physically touching while Kar and Mike seem to be really sparking off one another.

'You see,' Kev says looking towards me, 'I told you she wasn't lost or squashed or locked into a cubicle or on a bus back home!'

I laugh with them and even join in the conversation for a while. About twenty minutes later I'm still listening to the lads going on about the match when I see her wading through the crowd towards the doors. I watch her leave, alone. She's going, I think, and I'm never going to see her again. That little voice in my head starts niggling, telling me to follow her, to let her know how I feel. It persuades me that once we're alone she'll be back to the way she was.

'I'll be back in a minute,' I tell Kar quietly. She seems too interested in Mike to care so without another thought I leave as quickly as I can.

Outside it's cold and dark except for a few orange lights that give off a dull glow. I search around and see her halfway down the car park, leaning against a car, smoking. I check that there's no one around before walking towards her.

'Hey, Flick,' she says carelessly. She flashes a brilliant smile. 'Fancy meeting you out here.' I smile back. 'You aren't by any chance following me, are you?' she continues.

'Yeah, well, I saw you coming out and ...' I falter.

'And?' she asks, raising an eyebrow and dragging on her cigarette.

I shrug, then gulp, 'I just wanted to talk,' I say quickly.

'About what?' she persists.

'I dunno.'

'Fancy a cigarette?' she asks.

'Yeah, sure,' I say and reach for one.

'You know you can't do blow-backs with ordinary cigs,' she says.

'Ha ha,' I say as I light it. There's silence as she stares past me into the darkness. 'I was really hurt by what you said inside,' I say quickly, before taking another drag.

'Ah, relax,' she says.

'I'm sure you wouldn't like people to talk about your family that way ...'

'My family are all dumbasses and anyone can say what they want about them; I couldn't give a damn!' she replies bitterly. She looks at her watch. 'So,' she smiles, the bitterness gone just as quickly as it came, 'you liked our little tête-à-tête the other week?'

I look at her, wondering if she is just playing games with me or whether she honestly wants to know. I shrug. 'Yeah,' I say.

She leans towards me until her face is so close to mine. 'Oh yeah?' she whispers, a smile on her face. 'How much?'

'This much,' I whisper and I kiss her. She kisses me back and I immediately forgive her everything. 'I love you,' I breathe after a moment. I don't wait for a reply but kiss her gently again.

She pulls away from me and takes a drag of her ash-laden cigarette before flicking it away. I furrow my brow and stare at her, wondering what's wrong. A noise distracts me, but it's just some couple leaving the club. I turn back towards her with a smile.

'So you're definitely a lezzer?' she asks. The smile is frozen to my face but I'm cringing at her abrupt tone.

'Well, I definitely like you,' I say, hoping she's just looking for reassurance, 'and I hope you like me.'

She raises her eyebrows and I feel the hairs on my neck and arms prickle.

'You're pretty,' she says, taking another drag, 'but you're *so* naive. I mean, look at you.'

I feel the muscles in my body tense, ready for a punch.

'You're only a little frustrated lezzer who thinks that just because a girl kisses you she likes you or is like you!'

I gulp and look around hoping no one can hear. My

mind is whirling. I want to cover my ears; I don't want to know what she has to say.

'I'm not remotely interested in you,' she continues with a sneer. 'The night we kissed I was going to shag your pathetic brother, but thanks to your archaic parents I ended up snogging you. You were, unlike me, in the right place at the right time! Tonight … well, tonight I was just curious. You say you've come all this way for Kev's match but here you are with me, fumbling around, not having a clue what you're doing and promising undying love!' She laughs and pulls on her cigarette again.

I stand frozen to the spot and instead of walking away I just stare at her.

'I mean, you don't even bloody know me and you're telling me you love me!' she says. 'But you know what I'd love to see?' She pauses and looks into my face. 'Your parents' faces, especially your mother's – and Kev's – when you tell them you're a lezzer.' She laughs.

'I'm not,' I say. 'I like guys too.' I try to sound convinced but I can feel the tears welling up inside me.

'Right … you're bisexual,' she sneers, 'except you've probably never even shagged a guy or you've just snogged them to prove to the girls that you're one of them.' She flicks the ash from her cigarette onto the car bonnet. 'I know your type!' she scoffs.

I feel like she's looking into my soul and I want to run away but can't.

'I thought you liked me,' I finally snivel. She just looks at me. 'Why the hell did you kiss me?' I ask.

She leans in really close to me and waits. My eyes flicker towards her as I feel her lips touch mine so softly that for a second I'm not sure whether she's kissing me or not. I taste her caramel breath. After a moment she stops and whispers in my ear, 'Cause I want to see how much you can take.'

Somewhere behind us car wheels crunch on gravel. She stops and we watch as a large silver Mercedes swerves around in the yard. For a moment it's headlights blind us. I shield my eyes while Becks looks away. The lights give a quick flash. She looks back towards it.

'Well here's my lift!' she says.

'Oh ...'

She smiles and puts her bag on her shoulder, ready to walk away without a second look.

'See ya,' I whisper.

'No, you won't ... unless you're going to start stalking me,' she adds with a laugh.

The hurt sticks in my throat.

'Ah, lighten up,' she says, 'you take it too seriously.'

She stands and fixes herself then bends and kisses me full on the lips again. I don't pull away, but close my eyes and kiss her back. After a moment she stops, takes another drag of her cigarette then turns and walks away. She stops by the passenger door, casually finishes her cigarette and flicks it away before looking towards me one more time.

'Go home, Flick; I'm sure there are plenty of innocent little schoolgirls there who'll do whatever you want them to and who'll tell you they love you every single day!' she says, sliding into the passenger seat. The car's tyres skid on the gravel and it speeds away. I stand there watching her and the red tail-lights disappear.

CHAPTER 10

I don't know how long I stand there. After a while I think of the others waiting and wondering and I know I have to move. I don't want to see them or talk to them but even as I think it I begin walking back towards the door. I know now that there's only one thing to do: I'm going to completely forget about Becks and every other girl. It's guys and *only* guys I'm interested in and boy, am I going to prove it tonight!

'Sorry, sorry, sorry,' I say, 'I was being chatted up and couldn't get away!'

'So where is he?' Kar asks, giving me a weird look.

'Um, somewhere over there,' I say. 'I've managed to escape.'

'Right,' she says.

I figure she's annoyed that I've interrupted them so I glance towards Kev, thinking I could chat with him and Fee but they're snogging the faces off one another. The other alternative is to go walkabout and find myself some talent. I look at the gangs of lads laughing and drinking around me and every molecule in my body fills with dread. So instead of doing what I had promised, I end up staying with Kar and Mike and, of course, I drink and drink and drink.

'So, what's she like?' Mike asks me as Kar heads off to the loo.

'The best,' I slur. 'She's really funny in a sarcastic kind of way but you better not get on the wrong side of her – boy oh boy, some people that have crossed her haven't lived to tell the tale!'

'I better stick with you, so!' He comes a little closer.

'No, no, don't do that; she's lovely, just your sort … Me, I'm boring and dull and –'

'Just what I like,' he laughs and he's pulling me away after him, past what seems to have become a makeshift dance floor and into a dark corner.

'Shouldn't we wait for Kar?'

'We'll go back in a minute; you're not Siamese twins you know,' he says, staring at me. Before I know it he's kissing me and I just let him. When he pulls away it's to whisper in my ear, 'I've got a little present for you.' he says.

'What? For me?' I ask, confused.

He gives a quick look around then leans in closer towards me. 'Close your eyes, put out your hand and see what Mike will give you.'

I giggle and do as I'm told. He places something in my hand and closes my fist around it then he touches his finger to my lips. 'Shh,' he whispers and smiles.

I open my hand just a fraction; my heart is racing and I gulp as I stare at the small white tablet. A mechanical half-smile automatically appears on my face. Damn, I think, what the hell will I do now? I don't want the tablet – I don't even have a clue what it is but I know what they've done to people; you always hear the worst. I wonder if I can say no or even just pretend to take it. When I look up he's watching me intently.

'*Bon appétit*,' he says. Oh, to hell with it, I think and I pop the pill into my mouth and take a long swig of beer. 'So, have you done this before?' he asks.

'Yeah, ages ago,' I lie, 'but I'm not sure it was the real thing; it didn't really seem to work.'

'Oh, trust me,' he says confidently, 'this will definitely work!' He winks, pops a pill into his own mouth and washes it down with his beer. Within minutes my head is spinning, my heart's racing and my legs feel all wobbly. So many bloody people, I think, and they won't stop moving. My eyes start going all screwy so I close them and feel like I'm floating. The music seems louder than before and the blood in my veins seems to throb in time to it. Mike goes and comes back with more drink, some beer and water, and for the rest of the night we laugh and move in time to the beat and go crazy on the dance floor.

CHAPTER 11

'Flick … Flick.' I drag my eyes open and it still takes me a few seconds to recognise Kev bending over me. 'Come on, you can sleep in my bed with Fee, I'll sleep here on the couch.' I close my eyes again. 'Flick,' he calls, 'Flick!'

'I'm fine here,' I groan, 'just get me a pillow and blankets.'

'You sure?' he asks. I don't have the energy to reply so I don't. He's back in a few minutes, lifting my head and throwing a thick woolly blanket over me. 'Will you be OK?' he asks again. I barely nod, just pull the blanket over my head.

When I feel him pulling me up a little while later I want to scream. 'Go away,' I moan, 'I said I'm fine here.'

'Flick, it's me, Mike.' I don't reply. 'What kind of a gentleman would I be if I let a lady sleep on the couch while there's a double bed upstairs?' he asks.

I still don't reply, just silently beg that he'll go.

'Come on, gorgeous,' he says as he drags me up.

I give a small cry of panic.

'Flick, I'm not leaving you down here on the couch,' he grunts as he tries lifting me into his arms.

My eyes flick open. 'Fine, fine,' I snap, suddenly awake, 'just let me down!'

He eases me to the ground and I feel my way shakily towards the door, my head spinning faster and faster. I feel so sick. I collapse onto the bed the minute I get to his room. I can feel him at my feet, taking off my boots. I want to tell him to leave me alone but I can't so I just turn over and pull the blankets over me. I wake again when I feel him sliding into bed beside me.

'Aren't you sleeping downstairs?' I croak.

'Ah, you wouldn't throw a nice guy like me out of his own bed would ya?'

I'm too tired to argue or let it worry me so I just turn over and fall into a deep sleep.

The nightmare doesn't come for a long time. A shadow looms over me, pinning me down so that no matter how hard I try I can't move, then a constant pounding as the weight above me jerks back and forth. I try to get up, to turn away, but I can't. I feel warm clammy hands caressing me as beads of sweat drip onto my face and neck. I struggle to free myself but can't. I try to scream, to call out but suddenly his lips are on mine kissing me hungrily. He grunts in the darkness as he continues to move back and forth over me. I try to pull my arms free, to move but they're stuck, so I squeeze my eyes shut tighter, hoping it will make everything stop, and though it continues for a little while longer there's finally one last thrust before it fades away.

CHAPTER 12

Oh my God, oh my God!

I wake to find Mike fast asleep beside me. I rack my brains, trying to remember but the night's a blur; all I know is that I need to get out of here, fast! Instead I lie rigidly, afraid to move, wondering how I'm going to get up without waking him. My dull headache begins to pound and throb. Ever so slowly I sit up and edge towards the bottom of the bed then tiptoe towards the door. I turn the knob with excruciating slowness; it creaks as I pull it open. I stop and hold my breath then, without turning around, I squeeze out into the hallway. I stand and listen for a few seconds just to make sure he hasn't woken, but all I can hear are Kev and Fee's voices downstairs. I slip to Kev's room, grab my stuff and head towards the shower. It's only when I'm nearly dressed that I realise my boots must be back in the bedroom. I curse myself as I sit there before finally moving. Please God, just this once, let me get in and out without waking him, I think, as I creep slowly along the thinly-carpeted hall.

I hold my breath and push the door open. He's fast asleep. One of my boots is in the middle of the floor; the other, unfortunately, is under the damn bed. I bend and stretch in to grab it just as the bed springs squeak. I freeze, praying he'll stay asleep. I think about crawling further under the bed so he won't notice me. The springs creak some more and I hear him groan. Damn, I think, damn, damn, damn.

'Hey, Flick, is that you?' he asks croakily. I roll my eyes and reluctantly pull myself up.

'Yeah,' I mumble, 'I was just, uh … getting my boot.'

'What time is it?' he asks.

'It's after twelve,' I say, standing up. 'Um … I'm going to have to go,' I continue and veer towards the door, 'we have to get an early bus home this afternoon.'

'That's a pity,' he says, propping himself up on one elbow.

'Yeah, I know,' I lie, 'it's always the way.'

'So, how's the head?' He grins.

I shrug. 'OK, I guess. 'I better go,' I say again and turn away.

'Flick,' he calls, sitting up in the bed. I plant a smile on my face and look around reluctantly. 'I'm sorry about last night,' he says sheepishly.

'Which bit of last night?' I ask lightly, thinking it's the drink he's talking about.

He looks embarrassed and then he's speaking so

quickly and quietly that I'm sure I'm picking him up wrong. 'Um, you know … when the condom burst. I'm really sorry. I can't believe it happened.' He pauses.

I furrow my brow, confused by what he's just said.

'Will you be OK? Will you be able to go to someone to get the morning after pill … just in case?' he continues quickly.

It takes a minute for what he has said to sink in. I stand in stunned silence. My legs feel weak and my stomach starts doing somersaults. I reach for the bed and slump down.

'What are you talking about Mike? What condom?' I ask weakly. I wait. Let this be a joke, I think, just a stupid joke.

Now he's the one to look surprised. 'Don't you remember last night … when we were together?'

'We weren't together,' I say; 'I fell asleep straight away.' I stare at him, hoping he'll agree. 'I think I'd remember something as important as having sex,' I snap, 'so I don't know what the bloody hell you're talking about.'

'Flick,' he whispers as he looks worriedly towards the door, 'we both woke up during the night and it just happened. Don't you remember?'

'No,' I say as parts of my nightmare flash before my eyes, 'no.' I shake my head to try and get rid of it. I feel a choking sensation in my throat. I can't cry, I can't swallow and suddenly I can't breathe.

I run to the bathroom and puke. When I'm finished I just sit on the floor for a long time. My head is spinning and voices swarm around like a nest of angry bees. 'Idiot, fool, slut, you can't even remember having sex, you've been raped, there's no way you can tell, not now, not ever! I cover my ears to stop the voices and suddenly he's there again, standing over me.

'Are you OK?' he asks.

Do I look OK? I want to scream. 'Fine,' I say bluntly, as I scramble up and wash my face at the sink. There's some mouthwash there so I rinse and spit a few times. 'I have to go,' I say walking out past him and going back to the room for my boots. I pick them up and turn to leave.

'Flick, I really like you and I'd love to go out with you … if you want?' he says. I feel sick again just listening to him. I know he's just covering his back and I want to scratch his eyes out and tell him how much I hate him.

'I have to go.' He moves as if to kiss me but I push past him and walk away.

'Flick,' he calls quietly again, following me into the hallway. I stare back icily.

'Have you enough money … for the doctor?' he mumbles. Is this idiot trying to pay me off? I wonder as I grab my bag. Will money clear his conscience? Maybe he's afraid I won't go near a doctor, that I'll just hope for the best. I turn away and head downstairs.

I walk straight out into the front garden and puke again and again. By the time I stop my head is spinning and I'm shaking all over. I lean against the house and cry.

'Jeez, Flick, are you alright?'

I hadn't even heard Fee come out. I shake my head and wipe my hand across my face.

'Tell me,' she persists, 'what the hell happened?'

I can't stop crying.

'Flick, tell me,' she begs as she puts her arm around me. I close my eyes. 'Will I get Kev?' she asks.

'No,' I say. 'I'll be OK. I just need a few minutes.'

'So ... is it Mike?' she eventually asks.

I bite my lip. I can't bear to think of what's happened, of what he did and there's no way I want anyone to know. This is one secret that I can't ever tell – not Fee, not anyone. I shake my head as I try to get rid of him from my thoughts.

'Flick, you're scaring me,' Fee says, 'just tell me what's wrong.'

'I have to get the morning after pill,' I whisper.

'You mean you did it?' she asks, 'are you OK? Wasn't it good?'

I barely nod and just feel sick all over again. 'I just need to get the pill before I go home so Mam and Dad don't find out,' I say.

'OK,' she says as she glances at her watch, 'we better

go now. I'll just go say goodbye to Kev. Does Mike want to come with us?' she asks.

I shake my head. 'I don't want him to,' I croak. She turns away. 'Fee,' I call, 'you won't tell anyone, will you?'

'No, no-one,' she says.

Fee has hardly disappeared before my phone starts ringing and I instantly know it's Mam. It makes me want to cry all the more. Instead I take a deep breath.

'Hey, Mam,' I say, as casually as possible.

'Felicity! Oh, thank God. Where have you been?'

'W-what?' I stutter.

'Where were you? What were you up to? I rang twice last night and again this morning. I was really getting worried and I was cursing myself for forgetting Rita's number.'

'Jeez, sorry. I didn't realise you rang last night; we were watching some videos and I guess I didn't hear the phone and this morning I was probably asleep …' I trail off, hoping she won't investigate further.

'That's what your Dad said; he figured you were fast asleep and totally oblivious to me worrying that you were out all night drinking or doing God knows what … I suppose sometimes my mind just runs away with me.'

The tears start to stream down my face again and I stick my nails deep into my arm to stop myself from crying.

'Mam, I think my battery is going to go,' I blurt.

'We'll collect you about eight,' she shouts.

'OK, OK' I cut her off before she can say anything else.

Kev and Fee arrive out just as I hang up. Of course they stand kissing and whispering by the door. 'We better get going,' Fee says after a minute. 'So, do you wanna say a quick goodbye?' she asks, nodding towards the house.

I shake my head again.

'Come on,' Fee says as she grabs my hand, 'or we'll miss this train.'

* * *

'Kar just texted,' Fee says as we climb onto the bus.

'Oh, please don't tell her,' I say. 'I really don't want anyone else to know.'

'OK. I'll text her later and tell her to just meet us at the station. I don't think she had a good night,' she continues as I stare out the window. 'She hooked up with the goalie.' I nod. 'Flick, are you sure you're OK?' she asks.

'Yeah,' I lie, 'I'm just hung-over … and tired … and I dread the thought of going to this clinic.'

She starts to root around in her bag before handing me some painkillers and a bottle of water. 'So you had a good night … with Mike?'

'Yeah, yeah,' I say then bite my lip to stop the tears.

'Cool; he seems like such a nice guy. I'm really glad he snogged you instead of Kar.'

I want to scream, to tell her to shut up, to tell her what an animal he was. But I just stare out the window wishing I was anyone but me.

'So, what was it like?' she whispers.

I feel sick. 'Fee, I can't talk about this now; I really don't feel well,' I say.

'Sorry.' She grins. 'You can tell me all the gory details later.'

I retch.

'Come on,' she says, 'we're getting off.'

I sit for ages on some steps on the side of the street in the hope that my stomach will settle. Meanwhile Fee has gotten the number and directions to the Any Woman Clinic.

'We really need to go,' she eventually says, 'this could take a while.'

'OK,' I groan.

All the way to clinic she talks about Kev and what a great night they had and how wonderful he is. I try to look enthusiastic. It's only when she mentions Becks that I really start to listen. 'She really hurt him,' she says. 'Do you know that she two-timed him with the team physio? And he's some ancient forty-year-old.'

'Really?' I say in a half-hearted sort of way, although I'm not really surprised.

'Yep,' she says and relays the whole story.

All the while I'm wishing she'll just shut up. A dull ache has started in my head and the closer we get to the clinic and the more Fee talks the worse I feel.

CHAPTER 13

Fee walks straight up to the receptionist; I lag behind. 'Hi,' she smiles, 'we'd like to see a doctor please.'

'No problem,' the girl replies in a bored voice. 'Just take a seat and fill out the form. You're number fourteen.'

'Right ... thanks,' Fee falters, a little surprised by the pink form she's handed.

'There are pens on the tables,' the girl continues as we look around blankly. 'Please leave them back when you're finished with them.'

Fee looks at me and makes a face as we walk across the large brightly-lit reception area with its polished floor boards and tall green plants before plonking ourselves down on blue cushioned chairs. She hands me the form. I sit staring at it for a few minutes, sickened by the thought of having to tell them anything about myself.

'This isn't so bad,' she says after a few minutes. 'There aren't really that many people in front of us so we might not be here for too long.'

'Yeah,' I murmur. 'Fee,' I say, chewing unconsciously on the end of the pen I've picked up, 'will you help me? They're asking a million questions and I really don't want them to know anything about me … my name, address, date of birth …'

'Be careful of that one,' Fee whispers.

'Why?' I ask innocently.

'I think the age of consent might be seventeen, which means you're underage,' she whispers, 'so make yourself a year older.'

'Oh, hell, Fee, I really don't want to do this. Will we just go?'

She stares at me. 'Are you bloody mad? What if you get pregnant? Do you want a baby at sixteen? With a guy you hardly know?'

'No,' I whimper as I try to hold back the tears.

'You need that pill, Flick,' she says as she squeezes my hand. 'Just think, this will be over and done with in half an hour but if you ignore this and get pregnant you pretty much have a lifetime of living with the consequences.'

I look at the form again. 'Please, help me fill it out,' I beg.

'Hmm, the fact that they ask for your social security number means that they can probably access your details if they need to anyway,' she replies knowingly.

'Can't I just say that I don't have one?' I say.

'Everyone has one,' she says, rolling her eyes.

'Well, I'll say I've forgotten it.'

She raises her eyebrows.

'Please, Fee, don't give me that look,' I say. 'I really don't have a clue what my number is and even if I did, I wouldn't tell them.' I stare at the page again, 'So, what name will I put down?' I whisper. She sits staring blankly at the page. 'Oh please, help, Fee,' I beg again.

'I'm thinking,' she snaps, sick of my nagging. 'They say that if you have to lie you should stay as close to the truth as possible, then there'll be less chance that you'll be caught out.'

'I don't get it,' I say, getting frustrated.

'Well, what's your middle name?'

'Sarah, after Gran.'

'Write it down,' she orders. 'And what's your mother's maiden name?'

'Davis,' I say, beginning to write.

'What's your Dad's birthday?' Fee continues. 'And make out that you're seventeen so put in the correct year.'

I actually fill out the form fairly quickly, then under Fee's orders I study the answers so I won't be caught out. I start biting my nails as I read but it's impossible to concentrate. All I want to do is cry. I hate this; I hate being here. The buzzer sounds and a robotic recording announces number thirteen. My stomach churns.

Within minutes yet another door opens and a couple walks out.

I hear my number being called. Fee has to push me out of the seat. 'You'll be fine,' she reassures me as I stand and walk slowly towards the stark white door.

CHAPTER 14

I knock quietly before walking in and closing the door behind me. The doctor – a tall, thin lady – is sitting behind her desk. She gives me a brief smile as I say a hoarse hello and hand her the form.

'So, Sarah,' she says, smiling as she looks at it, 'what can I do for you?'

'I need the morning after pill,' I blurt out, hoping I can get it and run.

'I see,' she replies. 'And why do you feel you need it? Did you have unprotected sex?'

I wince and glow a bright red. 'The condom burst,' I mumble.

She nods knowingly. 'Are you in a relationship?'

'What?' I say, blinking furiously.

'Do you have a long-term boyfriend?' she asks more slowly.

'Yes,' I lie.

She looks at me for a few seconds. 'And is he here with you today?' she persists. I stare at her without saying a word. 'There are a lot of people who need the morning after pill after a one night stand, and not everyone is lucky enough to have a supportive partner … like you,' she explains.

'He had to work,' I say feebly.

'Of course,' she says, nodding her head. I can see she has me well summed up. 'Are you living together?' she continues.

'No,' I say and clear my throat.

'I just want to make sure you have someone that you can talk to, some support. This can be quite a traumatic experience, especially if this is the first time something like this has happened.'

'It is,' I say, thinking that I have answered at least one question truthfully.

'Now, when did you have sex?'

'Sorry?' I ask a little shocked by her question.

'When exactly did you have sex? Was it this morning? Last night? The day before?'

'Last night,' I say, wishing she'd just give me the damn pill.

'You see, Sarah, the longer you wait between having unprotected sex and taking the pill, the less effective it will be. After seventy-two hours it may not work at all.'

I nod obediently.

'So you've never taken the morning after pill before?' she asks.

'No,' I croak, 'never.'

'Well, you will take two pills now and two more in exactly twelve hours' time.'

I stare at her. Great, I think, this is very straightforward, if only she'd give me the bloody things.

'A lot of people tend to feel sick with this amount of hormones in their system so we recommend that you take an anti-sickness tablet an hour before taking the morning after pill.'

I nod and try to concentrate but all I want to do is leave.

'If you do get sick or if you have diarrhoea within the next three hours or within three hours of taking the second pill then it will not work as it will not have been absorbed into your system.'

'OK,' I repeat, wondering if I can ask for a second batch, just in case.

'You should also know,' she continues, 'that although the morning after pill is extremely effective, there is no guarantee that it will work.'

'What?' I reply, stunned. 'I thought …' My mind is in a whirl. 'I thought that once I took it everything would be OK.'

'Everything will be OK,' she reassures me, 'but you may still get pregnant.'

'I don't understand,' I say.

She smiles reassuringly. 'A lot of women become pregnant while taking the contraceptive pill and equally some women who take the morning after pill, for whatever reason, still get pregnant.'

'So even if I take this now and again in twelve hours, and even if I'm not sick or anything, it still might not work?'

She nods. 'I just need to give you all of the facts so you can make an informed decision.'

'And how will I know whether it has worked or not?' I ask.

'You will have to wait until your period comes. If it's late you should do a pregnancy test. When is your period due?'

I can't think. I haven't a clue when my last period was. I rack my brains and try to remember. 'I think it's due sometime next week,' I eventually say. 'So I won't know until then?'

'That's right,' she nods again. 'The tests that are out now are quite sensitive but if you don't get your period and your pregnancy test shows up negative wait a few days and do it again. It sometimes takes a little bit of time for the pregnancy hormone to show up within the body.'

My mind is spinning again; I'm totally confused by all of this.

'Try not to worry,' she smiles, then pauses a minute. 'It's also my duty to inform you that although there is no conclusive research yet, there are concerns as to the effect of the hormone within the pill on an embryo within the womb.' I feel sick; I have to get out of here. 'So if the morning after pill fails to work for you and you get pregnant the hormones from it may have a negative effect on your baby.'

'But …,' I say, then stop. I don't want to know anything else.

'I just want you to fully understand and be aware of what you're doing.' She pauses and I feel the tears welling up inside me. 'Are you sure you want to take the morning after pill, Sarah?' she asks, then waits.

What other bloody choice do I have? I think. 'Yeah, I'm sure,' I say. She opens a drawer in her desk and takes out the pills, explaining which is which and reminding me to take them twelve hours apart.

'OK' I nod, standing and taking the tablets.

'Sarah,' she says, just I'm about to go. 'How well do you know your boyfriend?' she asks.

'Sorry?' I say.

'Well, due to the fact that the condom burst you are not protected from any sexually transmitted diseases that your boyfriend may have,' she pauses, 'and vice versa.' I stare at her blankly. 'How long are you two together?' she asks.

'About six months,' I lie.

'Do you know if your boyfriend had any tests done for sexually transmitted diseases before beginning a relationship with you?'

'I dunno,' I say as the tears begin to well up again.

'And have you had any other sexual partners before this relationship?' she asks.

'No,' I whisper.

'I would advise you to have the tests taken for sexually transmitted diseases. Most of these can be treated successfully, if caught in time. We can actually do them now. It only takes a few minutes.'

'It's just … I have a train to catch,' I blurt out. 'Thanks anyway.' I turn to go, dying to escape.

'Sarah,' she says in a harsher tone, 'I think your health is a lot more important than catching a train, don't you?'

Considering Mam would kill me if she knew I was here, no, but I reluctantly hear her out anyway. 'Some of the tests, for example for HIV and syphilis, should be done in six months' time. So you'll need to return here then.'

'OK,' I agree, knowing already that I'll never come back. I watch as she gets a needle and walks towards me. Within seconds she's found a vein in my arm. I close my eyes and turn away as she pierces my skin and draws a tubeful of blood. A wave of nausea overtakes me.

'Now, I'll take a quick swab to rule out chlamydia.' She directs me towards the bed in the corner and tells me what to do. I close my eyes till it's all over then dress quickly. I really don't want to sit back down, to prolong this any longer, but I do. 'The results of the test for chlamydia will be back next week. If it's positive you'll have to go on an antibiotic and your partner will have to be informed and checked,' she explains as she writes down some notes. 'You will appreciate that we can't give the results over the phone but we can send them on to your address if you wish.' She looks down at my form. 'At 1 Primrose Lane?' She raises her eyebrows.

'It's over beside the college; it's really lovely,' I babble.

'Or you can come back in and collect them yourself.'

'I'll come back,' I mumble.

'OK. Any questions?' she asks.

Millions, I think, but there's no way I'm going to ask them. 'No,' I say shaking my head.

'I've taken blood, so you should sit down somewhere and get some tea and something to eat,' she says, looking at me, 'and take it easy for the next few hours.' I nod. 'Goodbye, Sarah, and good luck,' she says as I open the door.

'Bye,' I say lamely.

I stare in shock when the receptionist tells me how much I owe for the consultation, pill and tests. I empty my pockets, thankful that Dad gave me money for the weekend. Fee comes over and adds the rest.

'Kev wouldn't let me spend a penny last night,' she says proudly.

I try to smile and feel happy for her but really it just

makes me feel worse. I grab my bag and blink back the tears as I slowly follow her outside.

CHAPTER 15

I take the tablets and feel rotten all the way home and to top it all off Kar completely ignores me! She's peeved we didn't answer her texts and she tells Fee it's all my fault that she ended up with Noel who turned out to be a weirdo and a smelly one at that.

'His room reeked of stinking socks and really bad BO,' she moans to Fee. It's worse back in her house; we're just sitting down to some grub when her Mam asks her how the night went. 'Fee hooked up with Kev and is now obsessed with him. Flick hooked up with Mike who was chatting *me* up for most of the night and I hooked up with Noel who turned out to be a complete weirdo and who I never want to think about again, end of,' she snaps.

'Oh dear. I'm sure you'll meet a nice boy soon, darling,' her Mam soothes, 'try not to let it upset you.' Kar glares at her before storming upstairs while Fee and I stare at one another.

'I better go and check on her,' Fee says.

'Uh, me too,' I blurt, not wanting to be left behind

with Rita. 'Thanks for the lovely meal,' I stammer as I stand and look at my untouched plate.

'Yeah, it was delicious,' Fee calls back over her shoulder.

Kar has thrown herself on the bed and is reading a magazine by the time we get to her room. She doesn't even look up when we come in. Fee starts making 'talk to her' eyes at me.

'No,' I mouth stubbornly.

She clenches her jaw before reaching out and giving me a pinch on the arm.

'Look, Kar, I'm sorry for last night,' I begin awkwardly. 'Mike said there was nothing going on between you two … If there was, I never would have let anything happen.'

I can't say anything else. Thinking and talking about him makes me feel disgusting and dirty and sick. So I just stand there watching Kar read. I'm so relieved when I hear Rita calling to say Mam is there.

'I better go,' I say. Kar doesn't even look up. I'm racing along the hall trying to get to Rita before she says anything to Mam when Ryan walks out of the bathroom and I bump straight into him.

I gasp, stumbling backwards. He grabs me to stop me from falling and a wave of heat runs through me.

'Sorry,' he says, 'are you OK?'

'Yeah, yeah, I'm fine,' I say as he lets go and I make a move to walk on.

'So, had you a good night?' he asks. I shrug and drag my eyes from the floor to take a peek at his face. Those glittering blue eyes are smiling at me. I immediately look away embarrassed.

'I suppose so.'

'You don't sound too convinced,' he says.

'I guess I'm just wrecked … Mam's downstairs so I've to go.'

'We're going out to the Cove next Friday night,' he says quickly as I begin to walk away. 'So, do you fancy coming with us … with me, I mean?'

'Uh …' I can't think; I have to get out of here, away from Ryan, away from Kar. I look back towards her room, hoping she can't hear.

'Flick?'

'Uh, yeah, sure,' I say in the hope of making a quick escape.

'Great!' he says, his face lit up.

Oh my god, what the hell have I just agreed to?

'So will we meet somewhere beforehand?' he asks, moving towards me.

'Um … uh, I … I dunno,' I say, backing away. I only stop when I hit the wall but Ryan is still coming.

'Or will we just meet there?' he says.

His face is inches from mine and even though my mouth is open nothing comes out. My head is spinning.

I'm not surprised when I hear Kar's room door open

– it's inevitable, really: with me things can always get worse. Ryan turns immediately. I don't even bother looking back; I just duck under his arm and jog on down the stairs. Rita and Mam are chatting by the door.

'Are you all right?' Mam asks, looking at me.

'Fine,' I say, although I know my face is burning up.

'It really was so good of you to look after Felicity. It's lovely to go away knowing she's in such good hands,' Mam says to Kar's mam.

'Yeah, thanks a lot; I had a lovely time,' I quickly add. I practically push Mam out the door ahead of me.

'It was no problem,' Rita calls as we bundle into the car. I lie back against the seat, exhausted and close my eyes for a few seconds, grateful for the darkness.

Mam and Dad talk all the way home and then for ages after we get there until I think I'll never get to my room. The minute I do, I strip and stand under the shower with a nail brush and soap, scrubbing as hard as I can. It hurts like hell but I don't care, I just want to get rid of the feel and smell and memory of him. I lean my head against the wall of the shower and feel the water drumming against my shoulders and back. It gurgles as it swirls down the plughole. Eventually, still feeling dirty, I dry myself and head to bed.

I wake around two with an alarm ringing in my ear. It takes me a few minutes to remember the tablets. I quickly swallow all three, not caring that they should be an hour apart, and gulp down the glass of water. For the rest of the night I lie awake willing myself not to be sick and wishing I was anyone but me. By morning I feel lousy and persuade Mam I'm too sick for school; I can't face Kar or Fee anyway.

'I'll be back at five,' she promises, 'but if you're feeling worse give me a buzz.'

'OK,' I croak. I don't sleep or eat all day, just think of Mike and what he did to me. Even the telly doesn't drown it out. By the time Mam gets home at five I've had four showers and am feeling worse than ever.

'I'm taking you to the doctor,' she insists, even though I try to persuade her otherwise. Thankfully, she waits outside.

'It's a virus,' he tells me without even checking me out. My head spins – could I have picked something up from Mike? I wonder. Isn't HIV a virus you get after having sex? Isn't that the one that people die from?

'What kind of virus?' I ask.

'There are so many different strains,' he says.

Oh my God, oh my God … 'Can't you give me anything?' I ask.

He shakes his head. 'Not for a virus, just plenty of rest and fluids so you don't get dehydrated.'

'And then what?' I persist.

He looks at me, confused. 'Then hopefully you'll get better,' he says.

'Hopefully? You mean I might not? I could die?' I say.

He laughs as he writes furiously but he says nothing. I'm not convinced. 'Come back if it gets any worse,' he says, 'and don't worry, you'll be better before you're married.'

Oh my God, I think, I've probably got a lifetime illness on top of everything else.

go up to my room the minute I get home. There's no sign of my period and I'm scared to death of this virus thingy that I have. So I sit surfing the net for the next few hours hoping that it'll tell me I've nothing to worry about.

It doesn't. Instead it confuses me all the more. Nightmares of Mike and babies and painful deaths hound my sleep throughout the night. Tuesday is even worse; I spend most of the day in the bathroom, praying that my period will come and that the virus will go. By Wednesday, I'm utterly exhausted and none of my prayers have been answered.

'Jeez, you look awful,' Fee says when she calls in that afternoon, 'and I thought you were just pretending in order to avoid Kar.'

I shake my head. 'I don't think so,' I croak, wondering if I should tell her that I've probably got some fatal disease.

'So, did you get your period?' she whispers as she sits on the bed.

'No,' I say hoarsely.

'Oh,' she says, 'it'll probably come tomorrow.'

I nod and try to hold back the tears.

She starts going on about school, just to change the subject.

'How's Kar?' I ask.

She shrugs, 'she's still peeved over the weekend and the whole Mike thing and now she thinks there's something going on with you and Ryan too.'

'There's not,' I say with a sigh.

'So you prefer Mike?' she asks.

'No,' I snap.

'But you guys had such a great night … I know you're worried about your period but things like that happen. I bet you'll definitely get it tomorrow.'

I can feel the anger and hatred swell up inside me.

'Kev told me he's been asking for you a lot,' she continues with a grin. 'He wants your number. I bet he's going to ring you to ask you to go out with him. Wouldn't that be so cool? Imagine what the four of us could do …'

I clench my jaw to stop myself from screaming.

'Oh, damn,' Fee says, looking at her watch, 'I'm dead late. I gotta run. I'll talk to you tomorrow.'

With a slam of the door she is gone.

The darkness brings more nightmares, worse than before. I kick and scream again and again as I try to get away from Mike. But I know it's too late. My screams turn to cries as I realise I'm powerless to stop him. He'll never leave me alone! Somewhere I hear a soothing voice calling my name over and over again and telling me that everything is going to be all right, but it never will be, no matter what they say. When I open my eyes Mam and Dad are beside me.

'I thought there was someone here,' I sniffle.

'I know,' Mam says, 'but it was just a bad dream. There's no one here but us, and we're not going to let anything happen to you.'

It's too late, Mam, I think, it's already happened. I can't stop crying. I wipe the tears away but they still come.

'Why don't you lie back down and I'll stay here with you,' Mam whispers after a while.

I do as I'm told, promising myself I won't sleep, but like Mike, sleep is an impossible enemy to fight. When I wake again it's after six and I'm shattered. I tiptoe softly across the room to the bathroom.

Let me have my period, I pray. I check but there's nothing there. Ohmygod, ohmygod, ohmygod, this can't be happening, I think. I won't let it happen. I sit feeling sick and scared.

Mam interrogates me when she wakes up. 'Maybe there's something on your mind? Something that you want to talk about? You know you can tell me,' she says.

'It was just a crazy dream. I can't really even remember it,' I say.

'But you've had a few now and they seem to be getting worse.'

I bite my lip and try to brush her off and in the end she gives up and goes to get ready for work. I head downstairs and into the kitchen; I'm so hungry. Isn't that one of the symptoms of being pregnant? I think as I butter my third slice of toast; you start eating for two and become as big as a house in days. I shudder at the thought. All day I go from the kitchen to the bathroom to the sofa and to the TV. By one o' clock I've eaten three more slices of toast, an apple, two bars of chocolate, five jam and cream biscuits and I've drunk at least one carton of orange juice. I've also visited the loo at least fifteen times, and there is still nothing. I don't know which makes me feel sicker – the eating or the waiting. I throw myself back onto the couch and bury my head in the pillow. My life is ruined.

CHAPTER 17

By four o' clock the highways of my brain are clogged with depressing images of screaming babies and smelly nappies and runny noses. I feel even worse and I know it's another sign ... morning sickness. I've looked it up on the net; they say it can happen any time of the day and can last for weeks, even months! My life is officially over. I've set up residence in the bathroom, hoping against hope that something will happen. I'm up there, trying not to think the worst, when the doorbell rings. Who the hell is that? I wonder, as I reluctantly head down to answer it.

'Hey, what took you so long?' Fee asks as she pushes past me. 'Let me in; it's freezing out here.' I close the door behind her and follow her into the kitchen. I slump down on one of the chairs.

'Fancy a cuppa?' she asks, clicking on the kettle.

'Yeah,' I say, 'that'd be great.'

'So ... anything?' she asks.

'Not a bloody thing,' I moan as she walks towards me and drops the stuff on the table.

'Damn,' she breathes.

I plonk down opposite her and put my head in my hands. 'What the hell am I going to do, Fee?' I groan.

'Look, the week's not over yet; it might still come,' she murmurs weakly.

'Yeah, knowing my luck it'll come kicking and screaming in nine months' time,' I reply. We both sit in silence for a moment, thinking the worst.

'Ugh, I can't bear the thought of it,' I say, shaking my head, 'I'm screwed; I'm so screwed.'

'Very apt comment,' she laughs, trying unsuccessfully to lighten the situation.

I make a face but don't reply.

'There are some things you can do,' she suggests after a few minutes silence.

'Like what? And please don't mention gross stuff where I have to hurt myself; I don't do pain.'

'No, no,' she says, 'I think if you drink some gin and take a hot bath.'

'How much gin?' I ask looking over at her.

'I'm not sure,' she sighs, 'probably a few glasses.'

'I bet it would have to be an awful lot more than that,' I say sceptically, 'more like a bottle or two. So it might kill me but at least I wouldn't have to worry about being pregnant any more!'

Fee sniggers.

'It's not funny, Fee,' I say.

'I know, I know,' she says, unable to keep a straight face. Then she starts telling me of a time Kar had to take the morning after pill.

'How come I've never heard this story?' I ask. 'You haven't been talking to her about me, have you?'

'No, I haven't,' she groans. 'The whole world doesn't revolve around you, you know.'

I grimace as she tells me how Kar took the morning after pill then found a pack of her Mam's pills and decided to take them too, just in case.

'Jeez,' I say, 'that's mad. How did she feel?'

'Lousy I think, and it took ages for her period to come.'

'Can you imagine the headlines if something had gone wrong? "GIRL OVERDOSES ON PILL!"' We both laugh. '*Can* you overdose on the pill?' I ask.

Fee shrugs. 'Never heard of it happening,' she says as she munches through her fourth biscuit. 'I know one thing, though; she probably didn't need any other protection for a year after that!' We laugh again and when we stop I suddenly feel guilty.

'Be back in a minute,' I say, as I get up and go upstairs to check again. Of course there's nothing there and when I come down Fee's in the middle of texting lover boy.

'Well?' she asks.

'No,' I reply miserably.

'Any pains, cramps, rumblings? Anything?' she persists.

'Nothing,' I say.

'Hmm, well I might be able to cheer you up! Kev's just texted to ask if you're up for going out tomorrow night. He might be bringing a certain friend that you know home with him!' she says, wriggling her eyebrows. 'I said that you were still under the weather but all going well you might be OK by tomorrow.'

'What?' I shout, feeling sick and angry and dizzy all at once. 'I don't want to see him or go out with him or be anywhere near him.'

'Why are you always so bloody hot and cold?' she asks angrily. 'One minute you're all over him, the next you don't want to see him. Guys don't like that, Flick; they don't like games and I think you two could make a great couple if you just gave him a chance. I also think,' she continues, 'that you need to tell him. It might actually help; it's his problem too.'

I stare in amazement. 'One minute you're telling me the day's not over, I might still get my period and the next you're planning for me to tell him?'

'Well, I'm just looking at all of the options,' she replies defensively.

'Fee, I've absolutely no intention of telling him anything,' I say angrily.

'What?' she replies, shocked. 'But I know he really

likes you; he said so to Kev, and he really wants to make a go of this with you. I'm sure he'd stick by you if he knew about the baby.'

'Fee! First of all, if there's a baby in there, then it's my decision what I do with it … maybe I won't have to tell anyone about it.'

'What? An abortion?' she asks.

I wince, not wanting to say or hear the word aloud.

'But how? Where? And I've heard that loads of people have nervous breakdowns and get depressed after those –'

'Who?' I interrupt. 'Who the hell do you know who's had an abortion?'

'I dunno, I've just heard stuff,' she replies.

I snort loudly. 'Well, thanks for your support,' I say.

'I'm just looking out for you,' she says. 'If it was me I wouldn't get rid of it.'

'Well, Holy Mary, you're not pregnant and you don't have a clue what it's like so stop preaching to me.'

She's about to say something else but stops.

'Look, I better go,' she finally says, standing. We head towards the door. 'There's still time left for you to have your period. Maybe it's the stress and worry that's stopping it from coming. I know you don't want to go but a night out with a few drinks and a good bop might just get things started,' she says.

I bite my cheek but don't reply. I'm ready to kill Fee.

She turns and gives me a hug. 'It'll be OK, Flick,' she says softly.

Somehow I don't believe her.

The minute she's gone I head straight up to my room and crawl in under the covers. All I want to do is hide away and not think about Mike or the baby or anything but instead of stopping, the thoughts just seem to swirl around faster and faster, making my head throb. I feel so lonely and scared and I just don't know what to do.

Mam and Dad come home much later and when Mam comes upstairs I pretend to be asleep. She calls my name quietly, then just as quietly she sneaks out. I open my eyes as I hear her walking away and the tears start almost immediately.

I'm still crying when my phone starts to beep. I turn over and try to ignore it but it beeps again and again. I wipe my eyes and grab it, then stare in surprise. All the messages are from Kar and are all the same, which is weird considering she's supposed to be mad at me. The message is short and cryptic: 'Check out my Facebook! There's someone there you'll want to see!'

I log on and quickly click onto Kar's photos and scroll down through them. It doesn't take me long to find what she's talking about. The moment I click on the photo an image of me and Becks fills the screen. Underneath it the caption says, 'Who's Flick kissing in the dark?'

I stare at it, my stomach churning. This is the *end*. I sit staring in stunned silence while inside my brain is screaming. Oh my God! How the hell did she get this photo? How bloody long has it been here? Long enough for people to see it, I think, long enough for everyone to know!

The mobile's shrill ring jolts me back to reality. It's Fee. I automatically turn it off.

She knows, I think; she *knows* and so does everyone else, and Mam and Dad and Kev are going to find out. I know that I can never face any of them again … ever.

There is only one solution. I creep into Mam's en suite and go straight to the cabinet. I grab a container of pills and then head back to my room. I turn my laptop towards me, open a new Word document and type the word 'sorry'. Then I fill a glass of water and pick up a few tablets. I squeeze my eyes shut tight, too afraid to see or think about what I'm doing. I really don't want to do this but I know it'll solve all my problems so I just keep swallowing them.

'Please, God, may being dead be OK, may it not hurt or be scary or lonely,' I pray.

When the tablets have all disappeared I wonder if I have taken enough or whether I should look for more. I decide to lie down on the bed while I'm thinking about it. I pull the blanket over me and close my eyes.

CHAPTER 18

I wake up spluttering and coughing with some damn contraption down my throat that I try to pull out but can't. I start vomiting and can't seem to stop, over and over my stomach heaves and retches. Even when I think there's nothing left, I'm still getting sick. After what seems like hours it's over and I lie back exhausted on the bed. I close my eyes and try not to think.

'Felicity … Felicity.'

I can hear a voice in the distance but I'm too tired to respond. A light flashes in my eyes then it's gone, then tightness on my arm and people pulling at me and that voice is still there, calling me, hounding me. Eventually, reluctantly, I open my eyes.

'Felicity, do you know where you are?'

I try to focus on the blurred vision in front of me.

'Felicity, can you tell me where you are?'

I close my eyes. In the distance someone's talking, then another voice, closer.

'Felicity,' Mam says, 'can you open your eyes?'

I prise my eyes open and look towards her. I put my

hand on my neck; my throat feels raw and gravelly.

'Are you all right honey?' she sobs. Tears are streaming down her face. I can't think why. Dad puts his arm around her.

'She's going to be OK.'

All I want to do is sleep, and so I do.

It's dark when I wake up. I open my eyes and look around, trying to figure out where I am. A drip hangs from my arm and some sort of monitor is attached to me. I close my eyes and try to ignore my pounding head and sore stomach. There's a rotten taste of charcoal in my mouth and it feels dry and rough. I would give anything for a drink of water. It's a while before I hear the voices and I look towards the door. I can see Mam and Dad outside talking to a doctor. I close my eyes and turn my head away. They come in after a while and sit beside me, stroking my hand. I don't want to open my eyes, don't want to see them, don't want their pity and don't want to answer their questions.

'Felicity,' Mam says.

I don't respond.

'Felicity,' she repeats. 'Felicity, how are you? Are you all right?' she bends and kisses my forehead.

Then Dad comes over, bends down and hugs me.

'It'll all be OK sweetheart, don't worry about anything,' he whispers.

The tears slip down my face. I can see them looking at one another, wondering what the hell to do.

'Can you talk?' Mam asks as she squeezes my hand tighter.

'Yeah,' I croak.

I can see the tears in her eyes still.

'Thank God,' she breathes. 'Oh, thank God. We've been so worried, we –' She stops and looks at Dad.

Silence fills the room. I close my eyes and pretend to go to sleep.

* * *

When I wake the next morning it's to the sound of voices. Mam, Dad, Kev and Fee are over near the door whispering. I close my eyes, wishing again that the tablets had worked.

'Thank God you called in last night, Fiona,' Mam is saying. 'Otherwise we wouldn't have found her till it was too late. When I think of what could have happened …' She's crying again.

'Don't,' Dad says. 'We found her, she's safe and well and there doesn't seem to be any serious side effects; let's just be grateful for that.'

'How is she now?' Kev asks.

'Sleeping,' Dad replies. 'She needs it, so we'll just let her be.'

'Do you know why she would have done it?' Mam asks.

My ears prick up in anticipation.

'No,' Fee says.

'Neither do I,' Kev says.

'It must have something to do with those nightmares she's been having,' Mam says.

'Let's not talk about this here,' says Dad. 'Why don't we all go and have a coffee?'

'I think I'll stay with her,' Mam says. 'I really don't want her left on her own.'

'Cathy, we've been here all night and now it's morning, she's asleep and the nurses are constantly in and out checking on her … Anyway, we'll only be gone for ten minutes. Come on, you need a break.'

Within seconds I hear the door click closed. Then silence. I'm just breathing a sigh of relief when it opens again and feet walk towards me.

'Flick,' Fee whispers. 'Flick, can you hear me?'

I reluctantly open my eyes and look at her.

'I told your Mam and Dad I'd left my mobile in here so I can't stay long. How're you feeling? I was so worried.'

I shrug. I think of the picture and the fact she knows everything and I want to shrivel up and die.

'I wish you hadn't found me,' I croak.

'Well, I'm glad I did,' she says, 'and I'm glad you're OK.'

I start to cry again.

'I haven't told anyone anything,' she continues, 'and I won't, I promise.'

'It's not what you think,' I say, 'the photo, I mean; it's not what you think, I swear.'

'I know, I know,' she says. 'Look, stop worrying about it; you can explain later and like I said, I won't say a word about anything.'

'It's probably too late,' I begin, 'people will automatically think the worst when they see it.'

'No, no they won't, it's gone already and Kar's saying it was just a prank.'

I sniff and hang my head. 'Mam and Dad are going to hear, and Kev,' I snivel.

'No, they won't; they won't know a thing. Please, Flick, don't worry about it. We can fix it; we can fix everything.' She bends and gives me a hug. 'I better go … they're waiting on me. I'll see you later, OK?'

'Wait,' I say, 'I don't want anyone at school to know what's happened.'

'I can just say you have food poisoning. Loads of people come to hospital with that. What's the name of the Chinese beside the taxi rank? I'll say it was that one.'

'Thanks, Fee,' I whisper. She squeezes my hand then turns and runs after the others.

I'm staring out the window at a beautiful, bright blue sky and thinking of the mess I'm in when the door opens again. I instinctively close my eyes without looking around. A shadow looms over me before I hear her voice.

'Hello, Felicity, how are you this morning?'

I don't want to answer and yet it's like she knows I'm just pretending to be asleep.

'Oh, hi,' I say as I stare at the heavy-set nurse in front of me.

'I'm Kate and I'll be looking after you for the day so if there's anything you need?' Her voice and eyebrows rise simultaneously as she pauses, waiting for a response.

I give a vague nod. 'I'm fine,' I murmur. She smiles, and I know she's thinking that I'm a million miles from being fine.

'OK, well if you need to use the bathroom or anything,' she begins.

'Actually, yeah,' I say. 'Where is it?'

She insists on bringing me to the bathroom and waiting on me while I'm there. I'm so embarrassed. But within seconds I'm ready to shout for joy, to do somersaults around the room, to hug and kiss anyone I can find. Yes, oh yes, thank you God, thank you so much! I think as I sit and cry with relief. I've just gotten my period!

CHAPTER 19

By Sunday evening Mam and Dad are still glued to my bed. I don't think I've spent so much time with them since birth and we ran out of things to say hours ago. So they sit, hiding their worry behind smiles and pointless conversations (and, in Dad's case, the paper) while I stare out the window, thinking.

I've gotten my period; now if only I could come up with some story that would get me off the hook with that photo, then maybe, just maybe, things wouldn't be so bad. I rack my brain for possible stories: I was out for a breath of fresh air and this girl just came up and started kissing me; I was off my trolley and she looked like a he; it wasn't me! Nothing sounds even remotely plausible and I close my eyes with a sigh.

I wake in the middle of the night, dying to pee. Mam and Dad are nowhere to be seen so I figure they've gone on home. I buzz the nurse to unhook my drip and monitor and wait for ages for her to come. After twenty minutes I buzz again, but there's still no sign. When I'm finally about to burst I get up and unhook myself before making my way out the door and down the corridor. Most of the lights seem to have been turned off and there's just a dim glow in the hallway. To make things worse, there's absolutely no one about. I walk a little faster, wishing the toilets weren't so far away. I'm relieved when I finally reach the cubicle and have locked the door behind me. When I'm finished I open the door ever so quietly and just as I'm about to make my way back to my room I hear a small, frail voice in a room just to my left.

'Please, help me, please.' A shiver runs up my spine and the hairs on the back of my neck prickle. I look down the empty corridor, hoping to see a nurse, but there's no one there. I stand, not wanting to go near the room or the voice but I know I have to. I inch forwards really quietly then stop again just outside the door.

'Please, girlie,' the woman's voice says as if she knows I'm there, wavering.

As I push, the door opens with a creak. I hold my breath and look towards the bed. A little old woman is grinning grotesquely and pointing. I look towards where she's pointing, trying to make sense of it all. Suddenly he's there, in the room, inches from me. I scream and run. I try to shout for help but the words just catch in my throat. I feel him getting closer, can hear his running feet gaining on me. I dare not look back – if only I could get to my room – but the corridor seems endless and there are no doors to be seen. I feel him closing in. I'm sure his hands are stretching out towards me, ready to grab. I push myself forward with a cry. It's then that I see it, the dim light, the door ajar. I reach out my hand before swerving in and slamming it shut. I lean against it, breathless, but immediately he's there pushing against me. I watch as his fingers curl round the door and I know that I can't keep him out. I race towards the bed, pull blankets over me and scream and scream.

'It's OK; there's no need to be afraid,' he says, suddenly calm and quiet as he walks slowly towards me. 'I'm not going to hurt you, I promise; I just want to help.' But I know why he's here and what he's going to do and I won't let him do it again. His shadow edges towards me. The moment he touches me I go berserk. I box and hit and scream. I think I manage to kick him where it hurts.

'Relax,' he shouts, 'take it easy!' But I lash out all the more. Then just when I think I have gotten the better of him I feel more hands pinning me down, restraining me.

'No,' I shout again and again but I'm unable to escape and as I struggle I feel a sharp sting on my arm and everything turns to black.

CHAPTER 20

Mam and Dad are there early on Monday morning when the doc tells me I'm to be moved to the psychiatric ward.

'You mean I won't be going home today?' I say, shocked.

'Well, usually after this type of incident we like to monitor patients. Maybe you'd like to talk to someone about your nightmares and what's worrying you?'

'Couldn't I just go home and talk to someone there?' I ask.

He smiles but says nothing. I'm relieved when Mam corners him just as he's about to leave.

'Doctor Molloy, I know we've discussed this but may I have another quick word with you about Felicity?' she asks, moving directly in front of him.

I look from Mam and Dad to the doc, wondering when they had their little chat. 'I think it might be better for Felicity to come home with us rather than going to the psychiatric ward after all.' She pauses.

He raises his eyebrows.

'I, uh … we, uh, just don't want anything on her

medical record that may go against her when she's ap-
plying for colleges or jobs in the future.'

'Well, Mrs Costello,' he replies, 'the most important
thing now is to help Felicity deal with her depression
and her suicidal tendencies, wouldn't you agree?'

Mam flinches at the words as if someone has just
slapped her across the face, while Dad, who is standing
on the opposite side of the bed, looks up angrily.

'Of course,' she agrees through tight lips, 'but I have
every right to be concerned about how this, this, this –'

'Illness?' interrupts the doctor.

'Yes,' she agrees, 'how this illness will affect Felicity's
chances of pursuing certain career opportunities later in
life.'

'Felicity is a very lucky girl Mrs. Costello. She's had a
very near brush with death and has lived to tell the tale,'
he says. 'The important thing is for her to go on to lead
a full and happy life. I believe she can only do this if
she is given the proper care, as we discussed.'

'Yes, doctor, but will it be on her file for ever or
should I get her discharged and take her to a private
counsellor myself?' Mam asks desperately.

'I really would not advise that,' the doctor continues
a little more sternly. 'We have an exceptional psychiatric
unit here and it is imperative that Felicity gets the full
psychiatric care and supervision as well as the counselling that she needs. You saw for yourself last night
how tormented she is by her nightmares so she will

need to talk through her issues with a professional.' He pauses before continuing. 'Unless you feel qualified enough to give your daughter that level of support and attention?'

Mam doesn't reply so he turns abruptly and strides away. I flinch, guilty for causing all of this hassle for her. I quickly squeeze my remaining toiletries into the bag that she's just bought me but the damn zip sticks.

'Oh Felicity, don't do that,' she says, 'you'll break it.' Just as the words are coming out of her mouth the zip comes off.

'Oops,' I say, feeling my eyes well up. 'I'm sorry,' I choke. I bend my head and try to concentrate on reattaching the tiny zip but my hands are shaking and it's impossible to see through my tears.

'It's OK,' Mam whispers as she leans over and gently takes the bag and zip from me, 'I can fix it.' She sits on the bed and I sit down beside her and watch.

'Do you think they'll be able to fix me?' I ask quietly.

'Oh, Felicity,' she says, dropping the bag and zip and putting her arms around me. 'It's not about fixing you,' she says. 'There's nothing broken, but you do need to talk through the things that are making you so unhappy.'

'I guess,' I mumble, embarrassed.

'It's good to talk about how you feel … Maybe you're under pressure from school? Or something has happened with some of your friends?' She pauses. 'Well, no matter what the problem is, you can talk to me or Dad any time, about anything.'

She waits. I say nothing.

'Sometimes it's easier to talk with a stranger, so if that's what will help, then that's what we'll do,' Dad says.

I nod and Mam grabs hold of my hand. 'Felicity, I don't ever want you to think that there's no way out of a situation. We're always here to help, no matter what.'

'Yeah,' I say awkwardly.

'I guess what we're trying to say,' Dad adds, 'is that nothing is ever as bad as you think it is and we're here no matter how tough things get.' For a moment I let what they're saying sink in. I could say it now, quickly, without thinking about it or planning it, I think. It would finally be out in the open and maybe, just maybe they might not be so hurt or disgusted or disappointed and maybe we could all just go home together. I take a deep breath and open my mouth to speak.

'Someday you'll understand that, when you marry and have kids of your own,' Mam smiles, looking at me.

'Well, hopefully it won't be too soon,' Dad laughs. 'I know there are plenty of guys queuing up but they'll have to wait a while longer.'

They both laugh and I give a quick smile.

You see, that's the thing about my parents; one minute they tell me I can say anything to them, that they can deal with it, but the next minute they're landing all their expectations on me.

CHAPTER 21

The psychiatric unit is on the fourth floor of this new building. I wonder why they've put the unit up so high and how they ensure nobody jumps. Both my questions are answered by the time we reach the isolated wing; it's obvious they're keeping us well away from the other patients and although the walls are painted in bright pinks and yellows, the key codes on the doors and bars on the outsides of the windows mean that once you're inside, you can't get out. The one saving grace is that, for the moment, I have my own room, even if it's small with disgusting flowery curtains and a telly beaming down from a ridiculous height on the wall. They're much stricter on visitors here so Mam and Dad are made to leave and told to come back at six. I feel sick as I watch them walk away. Dad puts his arm around Mam's shoulder and I know she's crying. It takes all my resolve not to cry too.

One of the nurses explains that she has to check through my stuff. I'm totally peeved – I mean, I can understand her taking my nail scissors, and even my mirror and tweezers but my dental floss and earphones? Hello! She acts all nicey-nice, of course, and explains that some of the patients in the place could really harm themselves with things like that. She brings me down to the games room after that where there are people playing table tennis, as if they're on some sort of holiday camp and everything's hunky dory. Then she tells me about the group sessions for teenagers every day, where we get to talk about what's bothering us and where they give us advice on stress and peer pressure and stuff like that. Already I'm dying to get the hell outta here. I figure the best way to do that is to go to the damn classes as she suggests, smile a lot and act as happy and normal as possible.

Of course it's easier said than done and when Kev comes in at six instead of Mam and Dad, who are back talking to the doc, things take a nosedive. He stares out at the black clouds, his hands shoved deep in his pockets. His mood, like the day, has changed.

'Do you mind not saying to Fee that I'm here?' I ask. He nods. 'Just say they're keeping me in for a few more days and I'll see her when I get home.'

'Sure,' he agrees.

'So, aren't you going to say anything?' I ask after a minute.

He shrugs but doesn't turn around. 'Mam says I'm to talk about nice, happy things like the weather, which, as

you can see is crap, or football, which is also crap, or
… well, honestly I can't think of one other thing to say.'
After a minute he pulls back the chair and slumps into
it. 'Can I ask you something?'

A million probable questions race through my head.

'Why did you do it?'

I shrug.

'I don't think you know what you've done to Mam
and Dad,' he persists, annoyed by my attitude. 'They
blame themselves, you know. They think it's their fault,
that they're not good parents, that they're working too
much and aren't around for you more, that they didn't
see the signs.'

I bite my lip but say nothing.

'Aren't you going to say anything?' he asks.

'Yeah,' I say. 'I wish it had worked.'

Anger flashes across his face. 'When the hell did you
become such a selfish cow?' he snaps.

'Me?' I say, shocked by his sudden outburst. 'Me? A
selfish cow? I know it would be better for everyone if
I wasn't around; that's why I did it, you ass. Anyway
you're just peeved that all this has ruined your romantic
weekend with Fee.'

'Don't be so stupid,' he snaps, 'you haven't ruined
my bloody weekend, you've just ruined everything for
Mam and Dad.'

'Well, I don't know what you're so worried about; it's

not like you're going to be around. You don't come home for months on end and when you bloody well do you bring Becks with you and barely speak to any of us. Why the hell did you have to bring her anyway?'

'What the hell are you talking about?' he asks. 'What has she got to do with anything?'

'And the only damn reason you're home now is because of Fee so don't go calling me a selfish cow.'

I can see his nostrils flaring, his cheeks bright red, his eyes glinting with anger. But I continue to rant. 'You're just so pathetic the way you get so obsessed with every girl you go out with,' I say. 'That night after the match, you ignored me from the minute you saw Fee and left me stuck with Mike.'

'What are you talking about? I thought you liked Mike. You had a great night, and when we got back to the house I tried to look after you but you insisted on sleeping on the sofa. You were so out of it anyway I couldn't –'

'Exactly Kev, I was totally out of it and you left me with him so he could do whatever he wanted,' I say, tears pricking my eyes.

A confused look sweeps across his face. 'I thought you liked him. I thought that's what you wanted. Fee said that you were big into him and –'

'Yeah, well, I wasn't,' I interrupt again. 'I hate the creep; he was only interested in one thing.'

'What's that supposed to mean?' he says.

I shake my head and sniff back the tears.

'What the hell happened, Flick? What did he do?'

Shut up, Flick, don't say another word, I think. You'll regret it. Don't tell anyone and it'll all go away. Ignore it, pretend that it didn't ever happen, you'll be better off! He'll deny it anyway and you'll look like a fool, so just shut up! The tears are streaming down my face.

'I tried to tell Fee that I didn't want to see him or talk to him again,' I continue, 'but she was planning for him to come with you, promising that we'd have a great night,' I whimper. 'I didn't want –'

The door swings open in a wide arc and I stop abruptly. A tall, dark-haired doctor stands there.

'Are you all right, Felicity?' she asks.

'Uh, yeah,' I sniff, quickly drying my eyes.

She turns her icy stare on Kev. 'Excuse me, but may I see you outside for just a moment?'

'Sure,' Kev gulps and looks quickly towards me before heading out the door.

Damn, I think, the moment he's gone, what the hell have I said? I sit on the bed and curse myself for being so stupid. All the while I'm thinking what I'll say when he does come back, how to get out of it, but after twenty minutes my head is fried and I'm fed up waiting. I've just turned on the TV when the door opens. Instead of Kevin, the doctor has returned.

'Hello again, Felicity,' she says, walking towards me. 'I'm Doctor Rodgerie and I'm a psychotherapist. I'm going to be helping you over the next few weeks.'

'Hi,' I say distractedly, looking over her shoulder to see where Kev is.

'I sent your brother home. I think he needs to calm down and I think you need a little space as well.'

'Oh,' I say, surprised. She sits on the edge of the bed. Damn, I think, she's going to be here a while. She talks for ages, telling me about herself and what she does and what she wants me to do, like talk about stuff. I sit and listen and don't say anything.

Eventually she stands and opens the door. 'We'll chat again tomorrow. In the meantime, try and get some rest.'

My time in the psych ward feels like for ever. It's also scary as not only do I have more nightmares about Mike but I have a few about the other patients in here as well. So by half eight on Friday morning I'm dying to get the hell out of the place. I'm out in the loo, washing my hands when I hear Mam and Dad on the corridor near the nurses station, chatting to Dr Rodge (which is what I've now decided to call her).

'I just don't know what we're supposed to do.' Mam says in this worried voice. 'What if it happens again? How can I ever leave her on her own? Or go anywhere?' She rambles on, not waiting for answers. 'I found an old monitor – you know, like a baby alarm – in the garage yesterday but I'm sure she'll go hysterical if I set it up … and I've tried to take everything dangerous out of the house, or hide them at least – knives, tablets, razors, detergents, alcohol – and I know there're so many things that I've forgotten about. Can you think of anything else that I should get rid of?' she asks. 'What about the mirrors or clothes hangers?'

Clothes hangers? I think.

'Clothes hangers?' Dad asks curiously.

'Well, you never know what people will try to harm themselves with,' she snaps. 'Oh my God, I never thought of the string on the blinds in her room and Jack, I really think you're going to have to nail her room windows shut when we get home; she'd never survive a fall from an upstairs room.'

I lean against the wall and roll my eyes. Mam has finally lost it. Dad's going to love living with two crazies in the house!

'You have to stop fretting love; it's going to be all right,' he reassures her.

'No, it's not,' she snaps, before turning back to the doc. 'Should I check on her at night?' she asks. 'Should we try to talk to her about it all? Or just pretend it never happened? Maybe I should sleep in her room with her? I've taken time off work so –'

'Cathy,' Dr Rodge interrupts, trying to soothe Mam, 'I know this is really difficult for you; I know you're extremely worried; I know you'll do anything you can to protect Felicity, but you have to relax a little. You're stressed and that's not good for you or her. Try to get back into a normal routine.'

'Normal? There's nothing *normal* about this.'

'I know how you feel,' the doc replies.

'Do you?' Mam asks. 'Has your daughter tried to kill

herself too?' I close my eyes and cringe as I hear Mam's harsh words.

'No,' she replies ever so quietly, 'but I have worked with a lot of families that have gone through what you're going through.'

'I think Cathy … and I are finding this very difficult,' Dad says, 'and we want to do everything we can to make sure it never happens again. I suppose we're just so on edge at the moment,' he explains apologetically.

'I understand. Why don't we go into the office?' she suggests. 'We can talk some more there.' They walk a few steps down the corridor and Dr Rodge starts telling them about our sessions and how they'll continue in her private clinic in town over the coming weeks. 'Talk to Felicity,' she continues. 'Try to see her as the girl she was. You can't treat her with kid gloves or stick to her like glue; you just have to be there to support her. You have to trust her.'

'How the hell can I trust her?' Mam interrupts hysterically. 'I'm having nightmares about the terrible things she could do to herself. I'm just worn out worrying and she's not even home yet. Maybe she should stay here a little longer, just until we're ready for her.'

'Cathy, hon, it's OK,' Dad says. 'We're bringing Felicity home and we're going to get through this; I know we will.'

Mam doesn't respond.

'There are twenty-four hour call lines,' the doc continues. 'They're not just for people who are depressed and suicidal; they're for their families as well.'

'That other doctor was right,' Mam sniffles, 'I'm not qualified to do this; I don't have a clue.'

'You and your husband are probably the most qualified,' she says, 'you're her parents.'

Mam isn't convinced.

'And what do I tell the principal at her school? Her teachers? Our friends and relatives? I've been avoiding everyone and I know Felicity certainly won't want people to know what's happened. Do I let her back to school or should I keep her home? And for how long?' she raves. 'What are the signs that she's going downhill? How will I spot them? I didn't even know there was a problem the last time.'

'Let's go to the office,' Dr Rodge repeats as she steers Mam and Dad down the corridor. 'We've got some paperwork to fill out before Felicity goes home and I can answer all your questions there.' Their voices become fainter as they walk away until finally there's silence.

CHAPTER 23

'Have you taken your vitamins and folic acid?' Mam asks the minute I appear for breakfast the next morning.

'Yeah,' I say.

'And the St. John's Wort?'

'Yes,' I say again, plonking myself down and grabbing some toast. Mam and Dad insisted that I wasn't going on any of that medication for depression.

'I looked it up,' Dad said; 'it takes weeks before it has any real effect on the patient and there are way too many side effects.' Hence all this herbal stuff and vitamins.

'And how did you sleep?' Mam persists.

'Fine,' I say, rolling my eyes. I mean, she must know; she checked on me at least twenty times.

'You should get out for a good walk as well,' Dad says. 'Exercise is so good for –' He stops. 'Well, for everyone, really.'

'And you've been stuck in that hospital for so long,' Mam adds.

'Fine,' I say again, having no intention of it. When she starts talking about her sister's wedding, which is months away, I make my escape, back to my room where I lie on the bed and think through all of the things I need to sort out.

1) Being pregnant – I'm not! Yippee!

2) Picking up some STD from Mike – that virus thingy is gone and there's no way I'm ever going back to that clinic to get the results or do those other tests anyway so I might as well just forget about it.

3) Thinking about what Mike did to me – I'm never going to see the jerk again so I just have to get over it and try to forget about it … starting from now.

4) Getting Fee off my back about Mike – go out with someone else or tell Kev to tell Fee that Mike is going out with someone else or threaten never to speak to her if she ever mentions his name again.

5) Sorting things out with Kar – apologise again for being with that creep, Mike, and swear I'll never be with Ryan.

6) Everyone knowing about me trying to commit suicide and failing … miserably – only two people outside the family know at the moment: Kar and Fee. So I just have to persuade them to keep quiet. And what are friends for other than keeping secrets and covering up?

7) The picture of me kissing a girl … the picture of me kissing a girl – damn, damn, damn, this is where I always get stuck. Everything I think of sounds stupid and made up; It was a long lost cousin, a dare … Agh! I have to think of something, fast!

CHAPTER 24

At ten to four on Monday we're sitting outside the counsellor's office block, waiting. It's lashing rain outside.

'I'm going to run for it,' I say. Mam's about to protest and is grabbing the umbrella when I jump out and bang the car door closed. With my head down I race towards the large glass doors in front of me. They open automatically and without looking I run straight through them and into *her*. We both rebound and I instinctively grab her arm.

'I'm so sorry,' I gush as I steady myself and let go of her. 'I was trying to get in out of the rain and I – ' I look towards her and stop talking.

'No worries,' she says, her large brown eyes staring back at me. 'I really wasn't looking where I was going either.'

Then Mam's there behind me. 'Is everything OK, Felicity?' she asks.

'Uh, yeah, sure.'

'Hi.' Mam smiles at the girl before turning back to

me. 'Is this one of your school friends?' she asks, thinking we know each other.

'No,' I say, 'we … I just bumped into her.'

'Oh, are you both OK? Felicity, you really need to be more careful. I wish you had waited while I got the umbrella.' She gives the girl a quick smile before heading towards the reception desk.

I roll my eyes and she smiles. 'I really am sorry,' I murmur.

'Don't be; it's fine,' she says. I stand there for another few seconds. I can't think of a thing to say but I don't want to walk away.

'Well, see ya,' I finally say, knowing full well that I won't, and already I'm gutted.

'Yeah, see ya,' she says. I turn and reluctantly follow Mam.

'Her office is on the second floor,' Mam says. The lift is open and ready to whisk us upstairs. At the last possible second I look behind me and the girl is standing there, still looking at me. I catch my breath and just as the doors close I give a half-wave and then she's gone.

Damn it, I think as we stand squashed in the over-packed lift, why couldn't she have had a pile of papers that flew everywhere when I bumped into her and we would have both bent down to pick them up and stared into each other's eyes like they always do in the movies? Or maybe she could have slipped a card with her name and number into my pocket. I check my pockets just in case – there's always a zillion to one chance that she did so without my noticing. She didn't. Maybe if Mam hadn't been there I could have invited her for a cuppa, just to say sorry for being so clumsy. Maybe she raced over to the receptionist the moment the doors closed, found out what floor we're going to and is sprinting up the stairs now so she can be waiting right there when the door opens.

Oh God, I wouldn't want her there. I'd be mortified: Mam and everyone would be watching, I wouldn't know what to say. I'd have to pretend I had absolutely no interest in her and didn't know what the hell she was doing.

I start to feel hot and dizzy.

'Felicity,' Mam hisses. I look back at her and she nudges me forward. 'You're holding everyone up,' she says.

'Oh … oh, yeah,' I say, 'sorry.' Mam pushes me out into a waiting room with more apologies to everyone. I stop and look around. There's no beautiful girl, no words of undying love, just the same old boring world with a plush cream carpet and cushioned chairs. 'Is this it?' I ask gloomily.

'Yes,' she says, 'we're just to wait here; we'll be called.' I sit down on the nearest empty chair and look around; there are three offices just off the waiting room, which is pretty full. Dr Rodge's room is directly in front of us.

'Would you like a magazine?' Mam asks as she sneaks a peek at the other psychos around the room.

I don't have time to reply because just then Doctor Rodge opens her door and calls my name.

I've butterflies in my stomach and my legs feel weak and spongy.

'Hello, Felicity.' She smiles as she directs me towards two armchairs by the window and suggests I make myself comfortable. I head over but sit forward in the chair – people who relax always let their defences down and say way too much and I'm definitely not going to be one of those. For the next five minutes she reminds me that she's here to help and that we can sort out my problems by talking through them.

'So, how are you?' she asks.

I clear my throat. 'Fine,' I say automatically.

'I know it might be difficult to talk about some things, Felicity,' she says with a smile, 'but remember I'm on your side; I'm here to help.' She pauses and looks at me while I bite my lip. 'Another reason people don't like to talk about how they feel about things that are upsetting them is because it makes them more real,' she continues, 'and that can be quite scary.' She smiles again and although I know she's right I've still no intention of telling her anything. So she asks me yet again about my family and friends. I'm as bored talking about them as

I'm sure she is listening but she still wants to hear more. I'm so relieved when the time is up. But just when I think I'm escaping for another week she arranges for me to come back on Friday for more torture. I reluctantly agree before heading out the door.

CHAPTER 25

By Friday evening, after another long and boring session, I'm wrecked and the weekend looms ahead like an endlessly dark tunnel. I sit at the kitchen table flicking through a magazine that I've no interest in. Mam is cooking; it helps her to relax and take her mind off things, so she's obsessed with it at the moment. I don't notice the silence till it's broken. And in one fell swoop Kev is back. Dumping his bag in the hallway, he barges into the kitchen.

'Hey,' he calls as he walks towards Mam and gives her a very quick hug. I can see relief and happiness flood her face. 'Well,' he says throwing his jacket on the counter and coming towards me. He ruffles my hair. 'How are you?'

'Fine,' I say. He dumps his wallet, gum and iPod on the table. 'You do know that you've left a trail of destruction behind you since you got here?' I say.

'Who, me?' he asks innocently. He opens the fridge and grabs a beer. 'Dad still at work?' he asks.

I nod.

'He rang a few minutes ago; he's stuck in traffic,'

Mam says. 'So, how was college? Did you get what you needed to do, done?'

Kev looks towards me then quickly looks away. 'Yeah, I sorted it.'

'Good,' she smiles. 'And how was training?' She's trying her best to keep the conversation going while Kev just wants to sit and say nothing.

'Grand.'

'And Mike?' I feel the hairs on the back of my neck bristle and I pull a magazine towards me and begin to examine it.

'Fine,' he says.

'Well, when things settle down and get back to normal –' She stops and visibly cringes at her choice of words. 'I mean, maybe in the next few weeks he could come down with you and you could all go out like you had planned.'

'Yeah,' Kev replies indifferently as I catch my breath, 'but what with exams and everything we probably won't get the chance and I think he's going away for the summer.'

I breathe a sigh of relief and release my tight grip on the magazine.

'I've really made a huge amount of food here,' Mam says to herself. 'I don't know what I was thinking. Felicity, why don't we invite Fee over for dinner? It'll be wasted otherwise.'

'Um …' I've managed to survive a full week at home

without seeing anyone and I was hoping to make it two. I look at Kev and then Mam, ready to make my excuses, but when I see their expectant faces I change my mind and grudgingly agree.

The evening doesn't actually turn out too badly though. Fee smothers me in a big hug the minute she arrives and we end up chatting like nothing happened. She does try and coax me to go shopping with her and Kar the next day. I scramble for an excuse but Mam agrees enthusiastically.

'It'll be great,' Fee promises, 'there's loads of cool stuff out.'

'I'm skint,' I say weakly.

'I'll give you an advance,' Mam insists. My feeble attempts to say no are scoffed at and I'm forced to give in. That night I lie in bed thinking of a story that will explain the photo. I rehearse it over and over, praying it'll work. Twice or three times during the night I hear the door creak open and even though I pretend to be asleep I know that Mam is there, still watching.

CHAPTER 26

At eleven the following morning we're sitting in this little café, drinking hot chocolate and eating muffins. I've persuaded the girls to defer the shopping as I'm dying to get my story off my chest and things have been *so* awkward with Kar since they arrived at my doorstep earlier.

'Look, I'm really, really sorry about the photo,' she blurts out the moment we sit down. 'I really didn't mean to… I mean, it was really cruel of me and it was only up for half an hour and absolutely no one saw it. I swear …'

'It's OK' I say, taking a deep breath, 'but I'd like to explain … about the photo, I mean. It's not what you think.'

'You don't have to,' Fee says.

'Yeah, forget about it,' Kar agrees.

'No, I want to.' I take another deep breath. I remember Fee's advice on keeping as close to the truth as possible when telling a lie and hope that it works this time. 'So, that night after the match when we went to the pub, do you remember I went to the loo early on?' They both nod. 'Well, there was a queue so I went looking for other ones. I found some at the far end of the bar and when I was on my way back over to you guys I met Kev's ex-girlfriend.' I hear a sharp intake of breath from Fee. 'I didn't want to upset you by telling you that night,' I say.

'What did she say?' Fee asks, leaning forward. 'The girl is such a crazy cow; do you remember the stories I told you?'

'Jeez, yeah,' Kar says.

'Go on, go on,' Fee continues, nudging me.

'I don't even know how she recognised me,' I say, 'I'd only met her once,' I explain, looking towards Kar. 'Anyway, she grabbed my sleeve and asked where Kev was. I told her I wasn't sure, that he was about somewhere. Then she started going on about how she was still mad about him and wanted to get back with him.'

'What?' Fee screeches. 'No way! That slag; she bloody two-timed him with the team physio and now she wants to get back with him? Well, there's no way that's going to happen; no bloody way.'

'I'm sorry to be telling you all this,' I say again, 'I really don't want to upset you.'

'No, I want to know … I want to know everything, go on.'

'Well, she just kept going on and on about how she and Kev had such a great time together and were made for one another and how that physio guy was so old and boring and how it was such a big mistake. It took me ages to get away from her and when I did I took a detour around by the marquee in the hope of losing her.'

'Well done,' Fee says. 'I would have been fuming if she'd turned up. I'm sure Kev would have too; he can't stand her now.'

'Anyway, it didn't really work 'cause when I went outside for a ciggy later she was there and she started on about Kev again. I couldn't get away from her. Guys, she was so out of it, you wouldn't believe it, she was as high as a kite. She kept saying how desperate she was without Kev and how she wanted him back and she begged me to sort it for her.'

'Oh my God,' Fee says, 'and what did you say?'

'I just said that I wasn't going to and told her he was going out with someone else.'

'You did *not*!' Fee shrieks. 'Then what did she do?'

'She just kept begging me to get him back for her. Any time I tried to get away she'd pull me back and talk some more.' I look around quickly, making sure that no one's listening to our conversation. 'In the end I just got fed up and told her I had to go and she was better off forgetting about Kev. Then out of the blue she started kissing me,' I whisper embarrassedly. I turn bright red and look towards Kar. 'I guess you must have followed us out and saw that?' She nods. 'I was mortified. I tried to pull away but she had her hand at the back of my neck and wouldn't let go of me … When she stopped, she said, "That's for Kev; tell him I love him." '

'How gross,' Fee says. 'Are you all right? Jeez, she really must have been on something.'

'Yeah, I guess,' I say.

'What was it like?' Kar asks, enthralled.

'Awful,' I lie, 'I couldn't get away from there fast enough. Anyway,' I continue, 'next thing this Mercedes pulls up and she just walks off and gets into the car. Did you see him?' I ask Kar.

'I was just there for a few seconds,' she says, shaking her head. 'I dunno why I even took the photo or put it up … It's just I was so mad over the Mike thing and then I saw you and Ryan in the hall and he kept asking about you, and… well, I was rotten and I'm sorry.'

'I'm not going out with either of them,' I say, 'and I'm not going to.'

Kar nods but doesn't ask why and surprisingly nor does Fee. So we go round in circles for a while longer apologising and explaining and each in our own way hoping it will make things normal again.

'Come on,' Kar finally says, waving her Dad's credit card in the air, 'let's have some retail therapy; we could all use it!'

I'm wrecked on Monday after another sleepless night. But I decide to go back to school – not because I want to, but because Mam has no intention of going back to work while I'm around the house and she just won't leave me alone.

'I can drop you in,' she says; 'it's no problem.'

'That'd be crazy; you'd get stuck in traffic and everything. It'd be a nightmare. I'm walking with the girls,' I insist.

'Well, I was thinking that maybe I could have a quick chat with Ms Moran while I'm there,' she ventures.

'What? The principal? Why?' I say, whirling round to face her.

'We've been thinking that it's probably best if we tell her about your circumstances.'

'You're joking,' I say, shocked.

'She'll be totally understanding; I know she will, and Dad thinks that she'll be able to make sure there isn't any pressure on you with study and all that.'

'Please, Mam, I really couldn't bear the thought of

Moran and all of the teachers knowing what went on.'

'They can help, Flick; they're professionals. I really think it's crazy trying to pretend that everything's OK when you've been through so much.'

I start to cry. '*Please*, Mam, I'll be fine, I swear. I really couldn't bear it if they knew.'

'But Felicity, it'd be –'

'You don't understand! Everyone would know within a week; one of the teachers would let it slip or that nosy cow of a secretary would tell everyone.' I'm hysterical now and Mam just stands there looking shocked.

'OK, OK' she says, 'try to relax, Felicity, it's all right. I won't say anything.'

'You promise?' I sniffle and dry my eyes.

'Yes,' she reluctantly agrees. She's still asking me if I'm all right five minutes later and even though she's not convinced I make her write a quick sick note before I head out the door. Fee and Kar are standing waiting just outside.

'Let's get outta here,' I say as I give a last look back over my shoulder.

'Whoever thought you'd be so enthusiastic about getting to school?' Fee grins as she waves to my Mam at the window.

'Ha ha,' I say, giving her a dig as we walk on.

We get to school with a few minutes to spare and

I'm immediately surrounded by the girls, dying to know the gory details of the food poisoning and my stay at the hospital. I laugh it off as best I can and even give them the low-down on one or two cute doctors in there as well.

'You do know that there'll be a queue back outside the Chinese tonight,' Kar whispers. I laugh just as Cunningham walks in through the door. Within seconds everyone has disappeared from around me and silence reigns. I take out my book and breathe a long sigh of relief.

At lunch-time Katie and Jake – who got together at New Year's and who have survived eight long weeks of going out together – break up because she still hasn't put out. She's devastated and I'm thrilled because we spend the rest of the day criticising him and analysing every part of the failed relationship and no one pays me any more attention.

The minute school is over at half three I change into a hoodie and jeans and head towards Dr Rodge's office. I take a few detours so as to avoid anyone from school seeing me. Once I'm outside it, though, I stand and wait, hoping I'll see *her*. At two minutes to four I give up and head inside. I walk ever so slowly towards the lift hoping she'll appear from somewhere but the place is pretty empty. I knew she wouldn't be here, I think as I head up to the second floor. I grab a magazine, slump into a seat just beside the lift and wait. When Dr Rodge's door opens I automatically look up and then do a double take. I can't believe what I'm seeing: the girl, the one that I nearly knocked over, who has since knocked me off my feet is walking out of the room. I stare at her, dumbfounded, not really believing she's here. I feel tingly all over as she walks towards me. It all seems to happen in slow motion – I swear, it's exactly like the films and she's got this smile on her face and although I try to drag my eyes away, I can't. It's only when she reaches me and presses the button for the lift that I finally look back towards my magazine.

'Hi,' she says.

'Oh, hi,' I say looking back towards her again.

'Felicity, right?' she asks.

'Yeah,' I say; I can feel my heart beating so fast and hope she can't hear it too.

'My friends call me Flick,' I say.

'That's nice.'

Some guy comes up behind her and stands waiting for the lift; she twists round and looks at him quickly before turning back to me and making a face. I smile up at her as she moves a little closer, out of his way.

'I'm Joey,' she says.

'Oh, right, hi,' I say. 'So, have you recovered?' I ask. She looks back towards the office she's just left and seems about to explain. I turn puce. 'No, no, no,' I say hastily, 'I mean from me nearly knocking you over the other day … not anything else.'

She laughs and I'm silently kicking myself for being so stupid.

'Oh, I'm not so sure I'll ever get over that,' she says mischievously.

'Felicity,' a voice calls and I look past Joey. I hadn't even heard the door open but there is Dr Rodge, watching us both. I stand up abruptly, turning red with embarrassment and guilt.

'Oh, you better not keep that one waiting,' Joey whispers with a wink.

I give a short laugh. 'I guess I'll be seeing ya,' I say as I reluctantly walk away again.

'Yeah, see ya,' she says, still smiling.

I hear the lift doors opening behind me, but Dr Rodge is watching and waiting. It takes all my resolve not to turn and watch her go.

CHAPTER 28

'Are you all right, Felicity?' Dr Rodge asks, still watching me.

'Yeah, fine.' I walk towards the armchairs and sit down.

'So, how was the weekend?' she asks, sitting down opposite me.

'Fine,' I say again.

She raises her eyebrows and waits. I sigh and try to think of some worthless piece of information that will keep her happy.

'It was grand,' I say, 'Mam was a bit annoying.' Dr Rodge nods enthusiastically.

'She just wouldn't leave me alone for two minutes and I know she's really worried about me and all that but she's so irritating, so I'm trying to act normal and do things that I think will help her to relax about the whole thing, you know?'

'Hmm,' she says, 'and how do you act normal?'

Damn, I think, lousy choice of words.

'You know,' I say, 'by doing ordinary stuff … chatting and having fun and all that.'

'But you don't really want to do that?' she asks.

'Well it's not that I never do,' I say defensively, already feeling cornered, 'I just wasn't in the mood at the weekend; everyone needs time to themselves, don't they?' She nods in agreement. 'I think she and Dad expect me to be outgoing and in the middle of things all the time now and if I'm not they start looking all worried. Like this weekend, Mam wanted me to invite my friend around for dinner, so I did. Then Fee – she's my friend – well, she wanted me to go shopping with her all day Saturday, and although I didn't want to, Mam insisted that I should so I did that too. I'm surprised she and Kev didn't invite me to the cinema with them later that night.'

'So why do you feel you have to do what your family wants if you don't want to do it?' she asks. 'Couldn't you just talk to your Mum and Dad and explain how you feel?'

I shrug. 'I know they're worried about me and I want to show them that I'm OK … I just don't want them to send me back there,' I mumble.

'I'm sure if you explain your concerns to your parents, Felicity, they'll understand and support you.'

I nod. Yeah right, I think. 'OK,' I say, hoping she'll just drop the conversation.

'So, let's go back,' she suggests. 'You said your friend and brother are going out together? How does that make you feel?' she asks. I bloody hate when she asks me how I feel about things, I think.

'Are they going out together a long time?' she asks.

'Just a few weeks,' I say.

'Right.' She nods. 'You mentioned last week that your brother is away in college and never comes home … so how did they start going out?'

I bite my lip, wondering how I've gotten into this conversation and how the hell I'm going to get out of it.

'We were just out one night and they got together,' I explain offhandedly.

'So, he *was* home?' she suggests. I look towards the ground and search for an easy lie. 'Felicity, whatever you say is just between us,' she promises.

So I very quickly tell her about heading up to see Kev in college, the match and how they got together. 'You won't tell, will you? Mam and Dad would kill me if they knew we were there.'

She shakes her head. 'So how about you and your friend?' she asks lightly. 'Did you two meet any boys?'

'Kar always meets someone,' I say.

'And you?' she asks. I shake my head and stare down at a frayed patch on my jeans and start messing with it. 'So what did you do, when the girls met boys?'

I wonder if she thinks I was with some girl, if she knows … 'Well, I did sorta meet someone,' I say, backtracking.

'Oh?' she asks

'Yeah, my brother's housemate.'

'And are you two going out together?' she asks.

'No way!' She latches onto my comment and hounds me with question after question, all in her really nice voice of course, but she doesn't give up. She makes me so mad that all I want to do is cover my ears and tell her to shut up. Instead I just keep shaking my head and staring at the ground.

'Look,' I finally snap, 'I just don't want to talk about it.'

'OK,' she says and smiles, 'but I'm just trying to help. It's really good to talk things through.'

'Yeah, sorry,' I murmur, even though I'm not.

'Why are you sorry, Felicity?'

'Jeez do you ever stop asking bloody questions?' I snap. 'Do you want to know about him? Do you *really* want to know what he did to me? Do you want to know what the rotten pig did? He *raped* me. I was really drunk but he said I woke up during the night and we had sex and the condom burst. But I know that didn't happen. I know he raped me.' I burst out crying. 'If you ever tell anyone I'll kill myself I swear I will.'

She doesn't say anything, just moves her chair closer and lets me cry. Eventually she tells me not to worry, that everything will be OK. But I know she's just saying that. After a while she asks if I want to tell her the whole story, so I do, right from when we met.

'How are you feeling?' she asks when I've finished.

'I dunno. OK, I guess.' I look at her. 'You won't tell anyone, will you?'

'I won't tell anyone,' she promises. 'Is that why you're having nightmares?'

I nod and end up telling her about them too. When I finish I feel exhausted. She talks for ages and then tells me to come back on Friday and to ring her immediately if I need to talk or if I'm feeling upset or overwhelmed. She hands me her card as I stand.

'Thanks,' I mutter, heading for the door.

'Felicity,' she calls as I'm about to open it, 'it will be all right, you know.'

I nod even though I don't believe her.

I'm in the loo fixing myself up when I get a text from Mam – the sixth one today. She's right outside waiting, of course; I'm sure she would have driven onto the footpath and in through the doors if she could have – God forbid that I'd be left alone for a minute.

'That took a while,' she says as I slide into the front seat. 'Were you late going in?'

'No, I was there by ten to and went in at four,' I say, pulling on my belt and looking at the clock. It's nearly half five.

'So, how did it go?' she asks.

'Yeah, fine,' I say, then I stare out the window hoping she'll get the hint.

'You know, while I was sitting here waiting for you I saw that girl again,' she says.

'What girl?' I ask.

'That girl that you nearly knocked over the other day,' she says as she clicks on the indicator and pulls slowly out into the traffic.

'Really?' I ask, turning around and straining my neck to look back at the office.

'Yeah, she was waiting around there for a long time; I wonder if she's a patient – I mean, a client?' she corrects herself. She glances at me. She stops talking then and concentrates on the cars, crawling like tiny insects in front of her.

'So, where did she go?' I ask, trying not to sound too interested.

'Hmm?' she asks, distracted.

'Where did she go?'

'I don't know, I think some guy came along and they went off together. I got fed up watching them so I started reading that old magazine at your feet. They've some lovely recipes for chicken and lamb that I'm going to try,' she smiles as she glances at me.

'Great,' I say sarcastically.

She rolls her eyes and is about to say something but stops herself. I stare out the window and silently say goodbye to another dream as the first drops of rain begin to fall.

CHAPTER 29

It's amazing how quickly you get back into a routine. School's no different; it's like I've never been away. All too soon I'm back to my old self and dreaming my life away – Joey being top of my list. Fee and Kar are brilliant: whenever I'm called on and don't know an answer – which is, like, always – they whisper it to me or find some way to distract the teachers. On Thursday Fee purposely whacks her leg off the desk just to distract Reynolds, our Business Studies teacher, who's waiting on me to answer some question on income tax. She roars in pretend agony that makes me laugh. Reynolds, the ass, gives me a lethal telling off for being so heartless.

'How can you laugh at such a thing?' she asks, incredulous. 'I've a good mind to send you to Ms Moran.'

'No,' Fee shouts, 'it's fine, she's fine; Felicity didn't mean it.'

'What a gracious friend,' Reynolds continues, shaking her head and smiling as she looks at Fee. 'You could learn something from that,' she snaps giving me a final icy – as in, sub-zero – stare. 'Now, where was I?' she asks, looking back at the book. 'Ah yes, tax, now …' She surveys the class over her spectacles. 'Annabel Winters,' she says, looking at the girl directly behind me, 'can you tell me how I would calculate the income tax on a single male earning forty-five thousand gross pay per annum?'

I put down my head and cower behind Melissa Ryan, who's about three stone overweight, thank God. 'Thanks,' I whisper to Fee.

'You owe me big time,' she whispers back.

'How about I pass the IOU on to Kev? I'm sure you two could work something out.'

'Sounds good to me!' she says through the corner of her mouth.

We both go back to dreaming our separate dreams while Annabel Winters stares blankly at Ms. Reynolds, praying for some revelation or divine inspiration. It never comes.

On Friday I manage to change and get out of school in record time. I'm outside Dr Rodge's office by quarter to four, sweating profusely but hoping for a glimpse of Joey. Idiot, I think to myself as I eventually make my way inside, where Dr Rodge is already waiting.

Today her mission is to persuade me to tell Mam, Dad and the police about what happened.

'It was as much my fault as his,' I tell her. 'I should never have taken the tablet or drank so much or gotten into his bed.'

'No, Felicity, he shouldn't have taken advantage of you and you're under the legal age for having sex.'

'You don't know him,' I eventually shout; 'he'll twist it all around; no one will believe me.' I begin to cry. 'I don't want my Mam and Dad to know. I don't want *anyone* to know.' I sit sobbing for a while. 'You're not going to tell anyone, are you?' I ask again, thinking she could go to the police herself. I don't wait for her to reply. 'I'll do it again,' I say, 'I swear, I'll do something and it'll work this time.' She tries to calm me down, promising again that nothing I say will go outside the room unless I want it to.

'My first priority is you, Felicity,' she says quietly, 'I just want you to realise that by telling the police you'll stop him from doing this to anyone else again.'

I shake my head. 'I can't,' I say, 'I just can't. He'll get to walk away, they always do.'

The session eventually ends, but only after Dr Rodge has talked endlessly and analysed me to death. Of course I promise that I won't harm myself and will be in constant contact. Once I get out I head straight for the loos and plaster myself in make-up so Mam won't suspect I've been crying. I hear the lift door open with a ping when I'm on my way out and I race to get it, managing to squeeze in at the very last second.

'Hey Flick.' It's Joey. She's with a rather tall guy.

'Oh, um, hi,' I say breathlessly, 'how's it going?' I know I've gone bright red – maybe even bordering on purple – but I have absolutely nowhere to hide so I just smile embarrassedly.

'Yeah, great,' she says, 'Oh, by the way, this is Dave,' she continues as the tall geek flicks his greasy hair across his forehead. I think I hear a muffled 'hey' but I'm not sure. 'So, how are things?' she asks.

'Great,' I lie as the doors reopen. I walk out and stand awkwardly, waiting for them to follow me, but I'm secretly wishing I could just run away. I think of Mam outside, watching and waiting, and what she'll think when she sees us and the million questions she'll ask and aghhhh! This is such a disaster. She stops beside me, as does the world's best hair-flicker, and is just about to say something when I tell her I've got to go. 'It's just that Mam's waiting …' I trail off in embarrassment, feeling like a ten year old.

'OK,' she says but the smile has completely gone from her face and she looks a little bit confused or sad or something. I feel my eyes about to fill up and I bite my cheek and blink them away.

'Sorry,' I croak as I turn and nearly run out the door.

Of course Mam is waiting, full of questions that she is afraid to ask. I stare out the window feeling exhausted. All I want to do is get home to my room and cry.

CHAPTER 30

The nightmares come again that night, worse than ever before. I scream and scream till there's no breath left in me.

When I wake later the lamp is on and Mam's lying asleep beside me. I gaze at the alarm clock on the bedside locker: it's half four. The nightmare is still so clear in my head and although I want to get up I'm afraid to move in case I wake her. I wait a while, watching her. Then slowly, my gaze intent on her face, willing her to stay asleep, I edge gently from the bed.

I quietly close the bathroom door then turn on the shower. The water is hot but I don't care, I just grab some soap and a brush from the shelf and scrub until my skin is raw and sore. I dry myself quickly and throw on my dressing gown. I stare at the ground, concentrating on the cream tiles as I brush my hair, unable to look at the face that stares back at me from the mirror. I silently open the bathroom door and take one last look at Mam sleeping soundly before I sneak out and tiptoe quietly down the stairs and into the sitting-room, knowing that the TV is the only thing that will take my mind

off him. I switch it on and flick through the dismal
array of programmes. Suddenly the door behind me
opens and Kev is standing there bleary-eyed in his
boxers and a T-shirt.

'I didn't know you were home,' I say.

'I got in late last night,' he croaks.

'Sorry if I woke you,' I say.

'Nah, I couldn't really sleep anyway,' he lies.

'What's on?' he asks.

'Absolute drivel,' I say.

'You've had a shower,' he says, changing the subject
as he looks at the clock on the wall, 'and it's only after
five.'

'I couldn't sleep so I thought I might as well,' I
mumble.

'Do you remember last night?' he asks, tentatively
looking at the TV, and then at me.

'Not really, but Mam was beside me when I woke up
so I presume I had another nightmare.'

'You screamed a lot, Flick, and they couldn't seem
to wake you. Dad wanted to ring for help but I don't
think he knew who to call.'

'Damn,' I say, 'I'm really sorry. I don't know what
the hell ...' I trail off.

'And Mam just kept rocking you till you fell back to
sleep,' he continues. I just stare at the telly. 'So, do you
remember what it was about?' he asks.

I can feel him looking at me. I swallow and shake my head. 'No,' I say, but the word gets stuck in my throat and comes out weak and hoarse. I hope he'll change the subject. After a few seconds I hear a noise at the door. I look up and Kev is gone. I lean my head back against the sofa, close my eyes for a few seconds and sigh, wishing I could make it all go away – for good this time. Another creak of the door and my eyes flick open; there's Kev with a duvet and pillows. He dumps them unceremoniously beside me.

'If we're going to be up this early we might as well watch something good. Why don't you pick a Tarantino film and I'll be back in a minute,' he says. I go over and flick through the DVDs. *Pulp Fiction* is my favourite. It's old but I love it and the music in it is fab. I smell the sweet hot chocolate the moment he opens the door.

'You're spoiling me,' I say with a smile as I prop a pillow either end of the couch and spread out the duvet.'

'Never,' he says, putting the mug on a magazine beside me. 'Want anything to go with that?'

'Nah,' I say, slotting in the DVD.

'I'm in charge of the controls,' he says quickly, just as I pick them up.

I hand them over reluctantly. 'Please don't put it on loudly; I really don't want to wake Mam or Dad,' I say.

'Agreed,' he says, pressing the volume button down.

'I forgot about all of these stupid trailers,' I say, settling myself under the duvet. 'Wanna skip them?'

Kev seems not to hear me. He clears his throat. 'So, I actually did see Mike last week when I was back up in college,' he says.

Every muscle in my body tightens. My mouth is dry and I can't say a word but my mind is screaming. Don't let this be happening, *please* don't let Kev know what happened that night. I couldn't bear it. Please may he not start talking about this.

'Yeah,' he continues quietly, 'I asked him what went on that night.' I stare at the duvet cover wishing he'd just shut up. I want to cover my ears and close my eyes and go 'la, la, la, la, la, la' but I don't. I don't do anything. 'He says ye went to bed shortly after we did, that you were wrecked and you just conked out … He didn't sound that convincing.'

I feel sick to my stomach: sick at knowing that Kev has confronted Mike but also sick at Mike's pretend innocence.

'So I told him if he laid a finger on you ever again or even came within a fifty yard radius I'd beat him to a pulp.'

'No way,' I whisper.

'Yeah, so he told me to go to hell, that I was all talk. He said he could do what he wanted with whoever he wanted, whenever he wanted and that you were a big girl who could make up her own mind.' I feel my stomach heave. 'That's when I hit him … I think I broke his nose.'

'Oh my God!' I splutter. 'Kev, you didn't!'

He nods, then smiles. 'He'll be fine,' he says; 'he's just got two black eyes and a crooked nose now so he's not such a pretty boy!' He pauses for a moment. 'I'd say he'll be bricking it for these last few weeks of college and he'll be lucky if a broken nose is all he gets away with.'

'Oh, Kev, don't do anything else, he's not worth it,' I say quietly. 'Do you think you'll get into trouble?' I ask after a few minutes.

'Nah,' he says, 'he knows he's gotten off lightly.' We both stare back at the TV. The static image tells us to play the movie or watch the special features.

'Flick,' he says, 'I'm sorry I wasn't there for you that night and I know you don't want to talk about it or the things that are bothering you … but if you ever do, you know I'm here.' He pauses, 'I just don't want you to hurt yourself again,' he says quietly.

'I'm sorry I did that,' I whisper. 'It wasn't fair on any of you.' I can't bring myself to promise I won't do it again even though I know that's what he wants to hear.

He gives me a quick nudge with his foot under the duvet. 'Forget about it,' he says.

We both drink the not–so-hot chocolate and without another word he flicks the play button and relaxes back on the couch.

'Thanks, Kev,' I say as the credits roll. 'You're a great big bro!'

He gives me a wink and we settle into the film. He's fast asleep when I look back over at him ten minutes later. I sit staring at him, envying him and wishing I could just take his advice and forget about it all.

CHAPTER 31

Another weekend drags by, pulling me along with it. I pretend I'm coming down with a cold so I'm not forced to go out and end up spending most of the time in my room, playing my guitar. I'm actually getting pretty good at it but I suppose I'd want to be, considering all the time I've spent on it these last few weeks. The girls call over for a while on Saturday and I play them an old Janis Ian song, 'At Seventeen'.

'Wow, that was great,' Fee grins; 'you're really getting good.'

'It's a bit depressing though, isn't it?' Kar asks. She's lounging on the bed. 'And you're not seventeen.'

'You don't have to be to appreciate the song,' I say.

'Or maybe it'll take you till you're seventeen to get it right,' she says slyly.

I fling a cushion at her.

'I'm gonna learn some Joni Mitchell ones next,' I tell Fee.

'Who the hell is she?' Kar asks.

'She's this old singer-songwriter.'

'How old? And what's wrong with all the new stuff out there? Why can't you play some Kings of Leon or Green Day or Lady Gaga or someone like that?'

'She was around in the sixties and she sings really cool songs and I don't want to play other stuff,' I say defensively.

'Well there's no point sitting up here playing ancient depressing songs over and over; you'll end up just wanting to slit your wrists … or I'll want to slit mine,' she says.

'Shut up Kar,' Fee says and throws another pillow. Kar shuts up, as do I and Fee amazingly manages to keep a conversation going all by herself for what seems like for ever.

The rest of the weekend rolls slowly by. I lounge and sleep for most of it. I can see Mam looking at me, wondering, worrying, dying to ask loads of questions. But she says nothing.

On Monday I ask her for a note as I haven't done any homework and promise us both that I'll work harder this week. She grudgingly agrees, unsure of what to say or how hard to push.

Now that Dr Rodge thinks she's figured out what's wrong with me and what made me take the overdose she focuses in on the nightmares. She asks me to tell her about them and explains how they're manifestations of my inner feelings and fears. She discusses Mike endlessly, explaining that rather than the strong powerful predator I see him as, he's really only a weakling – a bully who preys on people physically weaker than him. She discusses how he manipulated me and how I've allowed him to control my life through nightmares and negative thoughts ever since the rape. In each session she helps me to visualise different scenarios where I see the real Mike and regain control of the situation. She also focuses on the guilt that I can't seem to rid myself of and explains that I need to forgive myself in order to move on. It's a long, slow battle and I usually have a good cry during the sessions but bit by bit I'm improving. By the end of April I can actually tell her anything... Well, almost.

I catch glimpses of Joey here and there over the weeks but I'm always too embarrassed or upset from the sessions to say more than a quick hi. So I'm really caught off guard one Friday evening when I've finished a little earlier than usual. I'm waiting on Mam when I see Joey walking towards me. Her boyfriend, the tall, lanky guy is with her but I can't, for the life of me, remember his name.

'Hey, Flick,' she says.

'Hi,' I reply, feeling a burning heat engulf my face. I look away, then back, then away again. They stop right in front of me and I just want the ground to open up and swallow me.

'You remember Dave?' she asks.

'Yeah, of course, hi.' He nods in reply.

'So, how are things?' she asks, oblivious to my embarrassment.

'Good,' I say, looking from her to her towering buddy. I shift uncomfortably, dying to think of something interesting to say. 'Great that it's Friday,' I say after a few seconds. It's a pathetic comment but it's the best I can do.

'Yeah,' she agrees, 'I'm so looking forward to this weekend. We're heading out to see The Cribs tomorrow night.'

'Oh my God, I love them!' I say excitedly, forgetting my awkwardness. 'Where are they playing?' She starts telling me all about it and then suggests I should go with them, that there are tickets left and what a buzz it would be. I start feeling embarrassed all over again. 'Well, I, uh, I dunno …' I say, eyeing Dave. I'm sure he's going to kill her for inviting me.

'Oh, come on, it'll be great, there'll be a crowd of us and you can bring some friends if you want,' she persists.

'Um, OK, maybe,' I say, thrilled that she's asked me. The car horn blows just as I'm saving her number. 'I better go,' I say and stuff my phone back in my pocket.

'OK' she says, 'see you tomorrow.'

'Hey' I say, sliding into the car beside Mam.

'Who was that you were talking to?' she asks.

'Oh, just that girl, Joey. I've bumped into her a few times, since, well, bumping into her that first day.'

'Oh,' she says, looking at me warily. 'So, what's wrong with her?' she asks.

'I dunno Mam!' I snap. 'People don't go around telling you what's wrong with them or why they're in counselling.' I roll my eyes and stare out the window while she pulls out into the traffic. 'I had a good session,' I say after a few minutes of silent guilt.

'Oh really? That's great,' she says, smiling. We chat the rest of the way home, or rather Mam chats and I say 'mmm' and 'oh' a few times but at least it's a start.

That night I persuade Kev to come to the concert with me. Of course Fee will be with us too but I'm hoping they'll be totally distracted with one another and won't really bother me. I also leave it to him to get around Mam and Dad. It's easier than I thought as it's the first time in ages I've wanted to go anywhere so they're actually ready to push me out the door.

CHAPTER 32

I go shopping with the girls the following afternoon because I've absolutely nothing to wear to the gig. I've been living in jeans and baggy jumpers for weeks.

'I think the St. John's Wort must be kicking in,' I hear Mam say as I walk back in the door to grab my forgotten purse.

'Mmm, and that counsellor seems to be working wonders as well,' Dad adds. 'Those nightmares are happening less and less.'

I cringe, knowing the nightmare of Mike will never leave me, but at least now I have them under more control. I slip back out unnoticed and call down to Kar's. Ryan answers the door and I blush the moment I see him.

'Hey, how are you doing?' he asks.

'Fine,' I say and wonder what he knows and who he's been talking to.

'Tell Flick I'm coming,' Kar roars from upstairs.

'Kar's coming,' he says and smirks.

'Thanks.' I smile back.

'So, I haven't seen you since you nearly died from food poisoning,' he says.

'Yeah, it was pretty rough … but I survived it.'

'Kar mentioned something about Whan's … but are you sure it wasn't my Mam's cooking? It's dodgy at the best of times.'

'Sssh,' I hiss, 'she'll hear you!'

He laughs. 'With any luck it'll stop her cooking.'

Without thinking I give him a dig in the arm. 'Be nice,' I warn him.

'Or what?' he says with a sly grin.

Just when I think I've gone back to an almost natural shade I turn puce again. I stare at the ground and feel his eyes on me.

'So … you ran off so quickly that night I didn't –'

We both look up the second we hear Kar pounding down the stairs.

'Great timing,' he says. 'But maybe I'll see you some time soon?'

'Sure,' I say.

'What?' Kar asks, opening the door wide and looking from one of us to the other.

'Nothing,' I say. Ryan ignores her. She turns and roars goodbye to her mother.

'Ow, that was my eardrum you just burst,' he grumbles as she walks past him and grabs my hand to drag me down the road.

'See ya,' he says hopefully.

I turn and give him a quick smile.

We shop all day and then I spend the evening in my room looking at myself in my new gear and wishing I could just wear my baggy jumper and jeans. Unfortunately Kev starts roaring about being late so I don't have time to change back. I can see Mam and Dad looking at my black shorts, tights, knee high boots and black t-shirt.

'Wow,' Dad and Kev say in unison while Mam gives a weak smile.

'I'm not sure,' I say looking towards her, 'maybe I should change. Is it a bit over the top?'

'Have you anything with a bit of colour in it?' she asks tentatively.

'It's nearly eight,' Kev says, 'you don't have time to change.'

'You do look lovely,' she says.

I grab my jacket and he shoves me out the door. Mam and Dad shout a last goodbye. Fee meets us at the bus stop and I vaguely mention that I might be meeting friends from counselling at the gig then immediately change the subject before either of them asks any awkward questions.

It's absolutely mobbed when we get to the gig and in an instant I realise that it's going to be impossible to find Joey.

'Any sign?' Kev asks.

'Nah,' I say in an 'I'm not really bothered' voice. The

band starts a few minutes later and they're amazing; it's way better than I imagined and yet for every minute of it I'm kicking myself for not texting Joey and arranging to meet her somewhere. Finally after an hour and a half they take a break. I look around and wonder if I should try to find her or whether there's any point. I'm still wondering when I feel a tap on my shoulder. I whirl round in surprise. Sure enough, there's Joey, right behind me, looking gorgeous. I actually don't know whether to laugh or cry.

'Flick, hi. Wow, you look great,' she says enthusiastically.

I give a quick smile, already embarrassed and conscious of Kev and Fee watching us. 'Oh, hi Joey,' I say with a nervous laugh.

'It's so great you're here; I really didn't think you'd come, especially when you didn't text.'

I give another uncomfortable laugh and look towards the others again before bumbling through an introduction. They all immediately start talking about the gig and how great it is and I just stand there, totally mortified.

'Hey, where's Dave?' I ask. 'Is he here?' She looks at me with surprise and confusion on her face.

'Uh, yeah, he's over there,' she says, nodding towards the stage.

'Great. Guys, do ye mind if I go over and say hello?' I ask.

Fee smirks.

'No, go ahead,' Kev says, putting his arms around Fee. 'We'll meet you outside after the gig?'

Within seconds we're lost in the crowd and the moment I lose sight of them I stop abruptly and turn towards her. She looks so beautiful. She has her short hair spiked and with her eye-shadow and mascara her eyes look darker than ever. Everything about her is so perfect.

'Sorry about that back there,' I say. 'I, uh, I felt like a right gooseberry and was just dying to get away, that's why I was asking about your boyfriend. I just needed an excuse to escape, that's all. So don't worry, I'm not interested in him or anything.'

Her face breaks into a smile of relief. 'Neither am I,' she says.

'What?'

'I'm not going out with Dave; we're just good friends,' she says.

I swear my heart does a double somersault there and then. 'Oh; oh right,' I say. Suddenly the lights dip and we're plunged into semi-darkness again. For a second I can't see a thing and I grab her arm, a shock goes through me the minute I touch her. 'Sorry,' I say, immediately pulling away.

'It's going to be impossible to get back to the others now,' she says. 'Is it OK with you if we stay here?'

'Sure,' I say as my heart nearly beats its way out of my chest. She turns back towards the stage and so do I.

I stare at the band, pretending to be mesmerized but all I can think of is how close she is to me, how even without touching her I can feel her beside me. I feel sick with excitement and nervousness and wish my stomach would stop doing flip-flops. The minute they begin playing, the crowd surges forward and we're pushed against each other; even if I wanted to move away from her I couldn't and in the end we both just laugh and jump and dance with everyone else. I want it to last for ever, to hang on to every second. Then they play some of their slower songs and I can't even bring myself to look at Joey, I'm so nervous. So I just stand there, millimetres away from her, with this lump in my throat and a wildly beating heart. When they've played their final song and their encore and the lights have come back on she suggests we go back over to her friends. Of course I agree. At least I can say I was talking to Dave, even if it's only for a few seconds. The gang are really nice and friendly and all that; they even ask if I'll come out with them.

'I can't tonight, but thanks anyway,' I say. There's no way I'm going to mention that my folks are waiting up for me at home so I just leave it at that.

'I'm gonna head as well,' Joey says. 'My grandparents are home from France tomorrow and I have to be sober and on my best behaviour.'

'You're French?' I ask. Looking at her dark skin and large brown eyes, I wonder how I hadn't copped before.

'Well, both my parents are. They moved here before I was born … but yeah, there's French blood running through my veins! Romantic, passionate, happy people, the French!'

'Fiery, quick-tempered, argumentative …' I add with a laugh. 'You're dangerous!'

She wriggles her eyebrows and we laugh. I wait another moment or two, trying to stretch out every last second before I have to go.

'Well, I guess I'll see you around,' I say. But then she suggests that we share a taxi home and I immediately think of Kev and Fee and what they'll think of it all and if they'll suss out that I fancy her. By the time I meet them downstairs my mood has completely changed and I can't even talk to Joey. I can see Fee looking at me with these quizzing eyes but I turn away and just ignore her while Joey explains the situation. They don't seem too bothered and within minutes we're on our way home. I practically jump into the front seat just so they don't suspect anything and then I hardly turn around for the whole journey home; instead I just sit and listen to them chatting about the band again. It's only when the taxi stops that I turn and look towards her and in a second she's gone.

Kev and Fee snuggle up together and I lie back against the seat wondering if Joey will ever want to see this Jekyll and Hyde that I am again.

CHAPTER 33

I wake up in foul humour on Sunday morning, raging about how the night ended. The more I think about it the more sure I am that she'll never talk to me again. I can see Mam watching my every move as I mope around the house, so after lunch I call down to Kar's. She was out on a date last night and I know all she'll want to do is talk about it.

We lie on her bed, gazing up at the ceiling, and I listen all afternoon without hearing a word she says. Finally she asks me about the band – or more importantly for Kar, the talent at the gig – so I give her a shortened version of the night. I figure it's best to mention Dave, the only male I can think of.

'So, you didn't snog him?' she asks.

'No,' I groan, more exasperated at her asking than at missing the snog, ugh! 'Anyway, maybe it's for the best: he's probably more messed up than I am,' I say, giving the same excuse I gave Fee.

'Maybe you'll see him at your session tomorrow,' she suggests, 'and you could invite him for a coffee; that's what I'd do,' she says.

'I know you would but I'm just not good at that sort of stuff,' I say.

'Trust me, if he likes you he'll be thrilled that you've invited him.'

'Hmm, and if he doesn't it'll be the most embarrassing thing, like, ever,' I reply.

'How could anyone not like you?' she asks. 'You're beautiful, funny, friendly –'

'Shut up Kar,' I say, giving her a dig.

'Ouch,' she says. I'm about to apologise but suddenly she's on top of me, grabbing my wrists and pinning me down. 'No one gets away with that,' she says. My heart is going crazy. I scream and laugh and try to wiggle away from her but it's impossible; she's so strong. 'Say sorry,' she says as she stares down at me. I stare at her over me. My heart skips a beat and I can feel myself go red all over. I gulp.

'Sorry,' I say as I try to laugh again but can't. She loosens her grip and I quickly shove her off me. 'I better go,' I say, sliding off the bed. 'I'll see ya tomorrow.'

'By the way, where's Fee?' she asks as I nearly break into a run for the door.

'Need you ask?' I reply, trying to sound cool and relaxed.

'Another one bites the dust,' she says. 'It'll probably be you next and I'll be left lying here alone, talking to myself.'

I want to go back and kiss her, just for a second, then

make her forget it ever happened. 'I don't think so,' I say in a hoarse whisper.

'It could,' she persists.

'Well, if it ever does, I'll come and visit you every second Sunday,' I promise. She grabs a pillow and throws it at me. I swing open the door and dodge it. 'Bye,' I shout and race down the stairs.

I go straight to my room when I get home. 'I've some homework to do,' I tell Mam, but I end up lying on my bed and staring at the ceiling, thinking for ages before finally writing a short text. It takes me ages to edit it and then I spend another half-hour wondering whether I should send it at all. Eventually I press the 'send' button, then wait.

After ten minutes I'm agitated; after twenty I'm demented. I check the sent folder on the mobile. It definitely went. I reread the text and check Joey's number then sit back and pray. When that doesn't work I decide to mess around on the guitar in the hope that that will distract me. For approximately one hour and forty-three minutes I strum, until I hear the double beep. I grab the phone and check. I really can't believe it when I read her text:

'Yes,' it says, 'would love to meet up for coffee.' I climb back onto my cloud and dream the night away.

race through Monday, a whirlwind of emotions. One minute I'm thrilled to be meeting her and the next I'm dreading it, afraid someone will see us and will figure it all out. There's nothing to figure out, I tell myself, I'm just going for a coffee to say sorry for being so moody after the band and after that I'm going to make sure I never see her again. I call and cancel my session with Dr Rodge and tell mam I'll get the bus home, then go and meet Joey in Chocoholics, this cool place outside town. We sit in the back booth chatting for ages about every-thing and anything. I know I should tell her I'm sorry for the other night and then go, I know I should, but there's no one about and I've still got plenty of time so I keep putting it off.

Then Joey blurts out that she wants to tell me some-thing.

'What?'

She takes a deep breath. 'Usually this isn't such a big deal; I don't know why I'm so nervous,' she babbles, 'but, well, people sometimes react badly … oh, I'm just gonna say it: I'm a lesbian.'

I look around to see who else has heard, even though there's no possible way that anyone has. 'Flick, did you hear what I said? That I'm –'

'Yeah,' I whisper, hoping she'll do the same.

'What's wrong?' she asks, looking around.

I can't believe she's being so blasé about everyone else hearing. 'I'm sure you don't want the whole world knowing,' I say quietly.

'Actually, I don't care about what the whole world thinks,' she says. 'I just care about what you think.'

What do I think? I think, oh my God I can't believe she's just come out and said it just like that to me, even though somewhere deep down I knew all along. I think I'd love to be totally alone with her so I could kiss her and tell her I sorta sometimes like girls too. I imagine us secretly meeting up and being together and then I think no bloody way. I think I have to get out of here fast. I think this is getting too dangerous, someone's going to find out. I look towards her and see her waiting.

'Gosh,' I murmur, 'it's good, if that's what you want.' My mind is a whirl. 'Have you told anyone else?' I whisper as I lean towards her.

'Yeah,' she says and nods, 'my family, all my friends, a few people from school and now you,' she replies.

I'm shocked and at the back of my mind that dream disappears. If people see us together and know she's a lesbian then I'm automatically guilty by association.

'You're kidding,' I say. 'You told your parents? How did they react?'

'OK, I suppose,' she replies. 'We talked about it a lot and they just want me to be happy. I think they thought it was a phase for the first few months but they're getting used to it now.'

'For the first few months?' I repeat. 'How long have they known?'

'About two years,' she replies.

'Wow,' I say. 'And what do your friends think?'

'They're cool; they don't see it as a big deal.'

'So how did you know?'

'I think I really always knew I was never attracted to guys, not even the good-looking ones or any of the big movie stars that the girls used to swoon over. When I was in sixth class there was this girl sitting opposite me that was so beautiful, I just used to sit and stare at her all day. When everyone else was thinking of kissing boys, I dreamed of kissing her. Once I even told her she was beautiful.'

'What happened?' I breathe.

'She called me a freak and told me to get the hell away from her!' She laughs at the memory. 'I kissed a few boys just to try them out but I never liked it. Eventually my Mum saw me crying one day and wanted to sort out whatever was wrong. I think she got more than she bargained for. I told her everything and I suppose it just went from there.'

'So have you been with girls?' I ask quietly.

'Yeah,' she laughs, 'a few …'

'And?' I say, craving more information.

And so she tells me about Carolina who was over on holidays from Mexico for three weeks and Lizzy who never stopped talking and Ann who went out with her for four full months before mentioning that it was really boys she liked!

'Wow,' I say, a little dazed.

'So really, what do you think?' she repeats. 'I mean, do you mind, me being a lesbian? It's just a few times when I've told people they weren't too keen on hanging out with me anymore.'

'No,' I lie, 'of course not; it's fine.' I really can't think of anything else to say. I look at my phone and check the time. 'Damn,' I say, 'I really need to get home.' I see her bite her lip and I feel bad but I need to think. I grab my bag.

'Here, I'll walk you to the bus stop,' she says.

'OK.'

It's only when we're walking out that I see heads turning towards us and I wonder if they know about Joey and if they think we're going out together. So once we get outside I begin to walk briskly.

'Hey! Hey, Joey!' We both turn around when we hear the voice, and I see a small, black-haired guy walking towards us. He was one of the guys that were at the band the other night.

'Hey, Neil,' she calls.

'Hi,' I say when he's closer.

'How are you two doing?' he smirks, raising his eyebrows. I cringe at the insinuation.

'Fine,' Joey replies casually, 'how did the other night go?'

'You missed a great night,' he says, 'but I'm sure you had plenty of fun yourselves!'

'We went home,' Joey says.

'Exactly.' He smiles, nodding his head knowingly.

My breath catches in my throat. Oh my God, oh my God, oh my God, I think, I have to get out of here. Without a word I turn and walk away. After a second or two I hear her running after me. 'Flick,' she calls as she jogs up beside me. I stop. 'Are you all right?' she asks.

'What the hell was all that about?' I snap.

'I'm really sorry,' she murmurs, 'Neil's just such an ass.'

'Joey, he's just implied that we're together, that we spent Friday night together,' I say, feeling sick all over again at the thought of it. I'm in a cold sweat. People are going to find out, I think hysterically. 'I'm not a lezzer,' I say, 'and I'll deny it if they say I am.' I can see the shock on her face. 'Why the hell would he think I was one?' I ask.

Her mouth opens and closes, but her words seem to be lost.

I turn and walk on. The bus has already swerved to

a stop and the crowd is pushing its way in through the double doors. I'm standing at the end of the queue when I feel her hand on my arm, making me turn round.

'Look,' she says, 'I'm sorry. I did tell them that I liked you but I said we were just friends … I swear I never implied that you were interested in me or that we'd get together; that's just Neil being stupid and trying to be funny. I'm sorry.'

I look towards the guy in front of me and wonder if he's heard. I just want to get away from here, to stop all this from happening; I should have known it was a bad idea. But then when I look at her I get this lump in my throat and I just don't know what to say or how to say it. I look towards the bus and the disappearing queue, then back at Joey and her big brown eyes and beautiful face.

'I've gotta go,' I croak, before turning and climbing on.

The doors slam shut behind me, severing all ties. I don't look back.

CHAPTER 35

Before I even get into Dr Rodge's office that Friday I'm dying to get away – I'm so not in the mood for it today.

'How are you feeling?' she asks.

It's only at the last second that I remember telling her secretary I was sick when I cancelled on Monday.

'OK,' I say, then start to blab about anything just to get off the subject. I end up telling her about the band on Saturday night; music is always a good topic – I could talk about music for ever and it makes me sound normal and teenagery. Of course I don't mention Joey.

'Sounds like it was great fun,' she says. 'Who were you with?'

'I wasn't with anyone and I don't want to be,' I say, immediately getting agitated.

'I meant who did you go there with?' she says quietly after a moment.

'Oh … oh, with Kev and Fee,' I murmur, embarrassed.

'I know you've had a bad experience, Felicity, and it could take quite a while to trust boys again. But they're not all the same, so just take things slowly and get to know them as friends first and foremost. Your feelings will change with time.'

'Right,' I say sarcastically.

'You don't agree with me?' she asks.

'Look, guys are immature juveniles that are usually only after one thing. I've absolutely no interest in any of them and I never will.'

She waits a moment scrutinising me. 'Have you always thought this or is it since the incident with Mike?' she enquires.

'Tom, Mike, it doesn't matter who it is, they're all the same. I don't even want to talk or think about any of them,' I say.

She sits quietly for a moment. 'You do remember what I said? Everything you say in here is confidential.'

I nod.

'It's good to talk about things, Felicity; bottling things up just makes us unhappy and feelings can be very hard to deal with and control when they're repressed.'

I nod again, thinking how right she is. Suddenly I'm tired – tired of trying to be normal, tired of pretending everything's all right, tired of being me. And even though I want so badly to tell her everything I just don't know how. A tear rolls down my face and then another and then another. So I sit for a while not saying anything and she does the same.

'That night when we were up with Kev in college,' I

eventually begin, 'I met his ex-girlfriend.' I sniff away the final few tears and tell the story of Becks, of how I fell for her from the first moment I saw her, how I organised to go to Kev's match just to see her, how disastrously the night had gone and how Kar had taken the photo and posted it on her Facebook page. I explain how I had taken the overdose because I couldn't stand the thought of anyone knowing and how I had fooled the girls into thinking that Becks was the one that was messed up, not me.

'I can't believe they fell for it, really,' I say as I pull at some of the threads on my jeans.

'Felicity, it's OK to like girls,' she says after a moment. 'It's natural.'

I put my head in my hands and shake it from side to side. 'No, it's not,' I say. 'People think lezzers are freaks and are weirdos.'

'Not at all,' she argues softly. 'I know lots of people …' She tries telling me all these positive stories but I don't buy it for a second. I've seen firsthand in school how the few suspected lezzers are treated and know I never want it to happen to me.

Eventually it's time to go. I close the door behind me with relief and promise myself that I'm never going to talk about it again.

Of course Dr Rodge has other ideas and I'm still listening to her going on about the whole girl thing the following week.

'You have to be true to yourself if you want to be happy; you do know that, don't you?'

Gimme a break, I think. 'It sounds great in theory, but it doesn't work that way,' I say.

'How do you mean?' she asks.

'Well, say I admit to my parents that I like girls, they'd be totally disgusted. I'd actually put money on my Mam having a nervous breakdown and as for my brother and friends they'd just think it was gross. And on top of that I'd be a laughing stock at school, so in my book being true to myself just equals my life being ruined.'

'You're right, Felicity, sometimes it's difficult for people to be open-minded. Parents especially find it difficult to accept who we become. They take care of us for so long, making our decisions for us and thinking that they know what's best for us. So it's hard for them to let go and allow us to make our own choices. A lot of the time parents have our lives mapped out for us; they know what equates to happiness for them and think it will be the same for us so they steer us in the same direction. When you come to a crossroad in your life and you don't follow your parents' directions it can cause anxiety and controversy. But even if your parents were to react badly it would be because they have your best interests at heart.'

I throw my eyes towards heaven disbelievingly.

'Look,' I say, exasperated, 'my Mam is great but that's when everything is perfect. Everything always has to be perfect: the dinner, the house, the kids, Dad – trust me, a daughter who's a lesbian is far from perfect!'

'I can understand that but I don't know if you're giving your parents enough credit. I think if you sat down and talked to them and explained how you're feeling you'd be surprised how understanding they could be.'

I stop listening.

'There are alternatives,' she continues, sensing my lack of interest. 'I could tell your parents for you,' she suggests.

I snort. 'It's not about who tells them; it's about them knowing. It's about how disgusted they'll be. It's about them thinking that they can fix me!' I stare again at the worn carpet before looking back towards her. 'Anyway, I'm a teenager; we go through all types of phases so it's probably just one of those. By the time I tell them it'll probably be all over and done with, so why bother? And you said yourself that everything takes practice,' I quickly continue, 'so maybe the whole being with guys thing is something that can be learned.'

She tries to argue, to coax me into telling, to give me advice but I'm not really listening any more and eventually it's time to go.

'Well, try to enjoy this phase while it lasts,' she says.

Her last piece of advice rattles around my head as I make my way downstairs. 'I'm not going to enjoy this phase,' I decide adamantly, 'because this phase is well and truly over!'

The weekend looks set to be long and boring until Kar has a major boyfriend saga on Friday evening and Fee and I are hauled down to her house to hear about what a total ass he is. He hasn't rung or texted her since Wednesday and Kar is used to guys ringing her at least once a day so this is definitely the beginning of the end. At nine o' clock Fee finally persuades Kar, after three hours of analysing, to ring him. He doesn't pick up.

'Maybe his phone is broken or lost and he's mislaid your number,' Fee says.

'Surely he'd have memorised it by now,' Kar says.

By ten, when the excuses are wearing thin, we decide to walk down to the phone-box at the end of the street. Fee figures if we ring from an unknown number we'll know if there's really a problem with his phone without him knowing it's us.

'Come on,' Kar says to me as she squeezes into the box beside Fee, 'and close the door, it's freezing.'

'I'm not sure we'll all fit; maybe I'll just wait outside,'

I suggest. She grabs my jacket and pulls me in. I'm literally on top of her. She smells of toffees and caramel and she looks gorgeous even when she's mad so I focus on Fee.

'Just ring,' Fee says, nudging her. She dials the number and waits while we watch breathlessly. Suddenly she slams down the phone.

'What?' Fee and I ask together.

'Oh my God, he answered,' she replies, amazed, 'which means he isn't dead or in hospital or hasn't suddenly gone mute and his phone is not lost and is in perfect working order.'

'Oh,' I say. I can see her lip quivering a little.

'Group hug!' Fee announces and before I know it we're all squashed together in an even tighter huddle. When we eventually separate I'm all hot and dizzy and Kar is even madder than ever. By the time we're back at her house she's sent a text breaking it off and after just two weeks Jamie is history. We lie around a while longer.

'Single again,' Kar groans.

'So am I,' I say. 'It's no big deal.'

'What about Dave?' Fee asks. 'Haven't you texted him? Aren't you two going to hook up?'

Damn, I think, me and my big mouth. 'One of the girls told me on Friday that Dave was caught a few weeks ago climbing out of his neighbour's window in ladies' underwear!'

'Lucky escape,' Kar says.

'For him or me?' I ask with a grin.

'You're definitely better off without him,' Fee agrees. 'Imagine having to share your undies with your boyfriend!'

'Let's not,' I say, relieved I'm off the hook once more.

CHAPTER 37

The following Saturday we're outside the games arcade in the shopping centre, eyeing up Kar's latest victim. We peer in past posters and machines.

'Can you see him?' she hisses.

'Um, I think so,' I say. 'Is he the guy behind the desk?'

'Yeah, yeah,' she says. 'Oh my God, isn't he just so gorgeous?' she asks for the umpteenth time.

'Yeah, defo,' I say but I can barely make out his outline in the darkened room.

'Is he the guy in the white T-shirt?' Fee asks.

'Yeah,' I say, but Kar says 'no'.

'Oops,' I say. 'Well, his friend looks cute from here as well.'

'You've got to be joking,' Kar snorts, looking in. 'OK, here's the plan, we go inside and we'll head straight for the car racing games,' she begins.

'Ugh,' I groan.

She gives me a filthy look. 'It's right beside the desk – ye'll get a good look at him; he'll get a good look at me,' she explains, 'then I'll have a go or two of the game. If he comes over to us, you guys just pretend you have somewhere to go and I'll meet ye back outside.'

We both nod and follow her inside. Of course it's a disaster from the beginning. By the time we reach the car game both he and his mate have disappeared from behind the desk.

'Where is he?' Fee says.

'I don't bloody know,' Kar says through clenched teeth, 'just gimme some money for the machine.'

'I don't have any change on me,' Fee replies.

'Neither do I,' I say apologetically.

'What? Oh my God, here he is!' she whispers. She's searching her pockets frantically for coins for the machine. 'Whatever you do, don't look round.'

Both Fee and I automatically look, catch his eye, then look away.

'Oh for God's sake,' Kar snaps.

Fee starts to giggle. I clench my teeth, determined not to join in but the moment I look at her I do the same. Kar storms out, disgusted. Still laughing, we follow her. The moment we're outside Fee roars with laughter. Kar pulls her to one side and tries to quieten her but nothing works. In the end we're all in convulsions.

'Hey, Flick.'

I spin round the second I hear the voice, knowing instantly who it is.

'Oh, Joey, hi,' I stammer. I quickly introduce her to

Kar and Fee, completely forgetting that she and Fee have already met. 'We were just in the arcades,' I babble, knowing she thinks we're total juveniles.

'Flick, we're going back inside,' Kar says after she rattles some coins she's found.

'I'll be there in a minute.' I look at Joey, not knowing what to say.

'Look, I'm really sorry about that day in the café and Neil and all that,' she blurts out.

'I'm sorry too,' I say.

'No, I know how you must have felt and I –'

Fee comes bounding over to us. 'He came straight over,' she squeals, 'and he's talking to her!'

'Already?' I say. 'That was fast. I better go,' I say to Joey.

'Yeah, me too. I guess I'll see you around.'

'Sure,' I say flippantly before turning back towards the arcades with Fee. I give a quick look back just as we reach the door but Joey seems to have disappeared. With a sigh I follow Fee inside.

* * *

Kar is still on a high over Mr Cute Guy when we meet up the next day. 'Oh my God,' she squeals as she flops onto her bed, 'Arnold's taking me out tonight and I've absolutely nothing to wear!'

'Arnold?' Fee asks with a smirk.

'Yeah,' Kar replies protectively, 'but everyone calls him Arnie. I like that; I think it's really friendly.'

Fee snorts with laughter. 'Wasn't one of the muppets on *Sesame Street* called Arnie? The really stupid one?' she asks.

'Ernie,' I say. 'It was Bert and Ernie and yeah, he was a bit stupid.' We both laugh.

'I mean, what the hell were his parents thinking?' Fee wonders aloud.

'They were probably thinking of Arnold Schwarzenegger,' Kar says sincerely and we burst out laughing again.

'Oh, shut up,' she says, 'you're both just jealous.'

'Hello! Don't think so!' Fee replies smugly. 'Remember Kevin?' They both look at me expectantly.

'I've got a date with Leonardo,' I offer.

'Who the hell is Leonardo?' Kar asks.

'DiCaprio,' I say.

'Oh for God's sake, Flick!' Kar says while Fee rolls her eyes in the mirror and starts trying on some of Kar's make-up.

'It's *Revolutionary Road*. I've never seen it and it's supposed to be brilliant.'

'You have got to get a life,' Kar insists.

'I *have* a life,' I say sharply, 'and just 'cause I don't want to go out one night –'

'Any night,' she persists.

'I've gotta go,' I say, suddenly standing.

'Running away isn't going to help,' Kar says.

'I'm not running, I've got homework,' I say.

'Right, like you're going to study on a Sunday afternoon? When have you ever?'

'Bye,' I call as I walk out the door.

'You going already?' Fee asks, suddenly zoning back into the conversation.

'Avoidance is pointless,' Kar calls.

I roll my eyes, turn and head downstairs. I'd take study over this conversation any day.

CHAPTER 38

I have a few boring sessions with Dr Rodge that week and the next. I'm not in the mood to discuss or to analyse but she seems happy to just sit quietly and wait for me to do the talking. I'm so glad to get out on Monday afternoon that I'm jogging down the front steps when I catch a glimpse of Joey walking towards the bus stop. I look towards her again but I lose my footing and stumble forwards with hands outstretched, hoping there's something I can grab to save myself. The something turns out to be a young guy on a bike.

'Watch it,' he roars as he swerves away from me. He's still shouting abuse when I land in a heap on the ground. I'm mortified and I try to get up straight away, before anyone sees me but the minute I move a dart of pain shoots through my ankle. Damn it, I think and try again to stand.

'Are you OK?'

I look up to see Joey staring down at me. Already I'm bright red. 'I'm not sure; my ankle's killing me,' I groan.

She helps me up and I suddenly feel all queasy and hot. The queasy feeling is because of my ankle; the hot part is from being so close to her. 'I'll be fine in a few minutes,' I say. Except I'm not fine, not even after a few minutes: the second I put any weight on it, it kills me.

'Is your Mum coming to collect you?' she asks.

'I told her I'd get the bus,' I say as I try to stand again. Then she orders a taxi and we sit on the steps, waiting. I focus all my attention on my ankle cause I'm such a coward and then the taxi is right there in front of us. She helps me up and into it and just when I'm about to say goodbye she slides in beside me.

'You'll need help when you get there,' she explains. I don't argue, just sit beside her feeling my heart pounding and butterflies in my stomach. I can't even remember what we talk about on the way home but before I know it we're there and she's helping me out and into the house and onto the sofa, and she's so close and for just a second longer than I should I hold onto her and wish that things were different.

'Right,' she says as I sit with my feet up, 'gimme a minute.' She disappears into the kitchen and arrives back with her arms full. 'One pack of frozen peas for your ankle – I couldn't find anything else – one can of orange, some chocolate and some biscuits – they say you should always keep your sugar levels up after something traumatic happens.'

She looks around then heads for Dad's armchair. 'One TV control … or one schoolbag if insanity kicks in and you decide to do some study!'

'I won't,' I smile. She smiles back at me then gently lifts my ankle and slides a cushion underneath. The smile disappears from my face.

'Thanks.'

Then she says goodbye and walks towards the door and the waiting taxi; before I know it she's gone.

When Mam gets home and sees my ankle she bundles me into the car and off to A&E. It turns out I've torn some ligaments and they give me crutches and some painkillers. Mam starts panicking when she sees me taking them. I want to tell her to get over it, that I'm not going to OD on them, but in the end I just keep my mouth shut.

Later, when I'm up in my room I hear them arguing downstairs. I sneak out to the landing and listen.

'I have that proposal; I need to be there,' Mam says.

'Well, so do I; I've management meetings organised.'

'Surely you could postpone them for the day?' Mam pleads. 'You *are* the boss!'

'Felicity will be fine by herself,' he insists.

'No, she won't. I'm not leaving her here; one of us needs to stay with her.'

I limp back to my room and close the door. Great, I think, just great; I'm under house arrest again!

CHAPTER 39

When I eventually make my way downstairs the next morning Dad's sitting at the kitchen table working on his laptop. Although he intends to stay home all day he's called into the office at one o'clock. He makes me a toasted cheese and ham sambo and promises he'll be back as soon as he can. I'm still in the same spot, staring at the telly when the doorbell rings at three.

'Who the hell …?' I hobble towards the door. Kar and Fee are standing there beaming at me.

'We had last class free,' Fee says.

'Deadly,' Kar says, seeing my crutches, 'let me have a go.'

I limp back to the couch and then hand them to her. She spends ages parading around the sitting-room while Fee goes on and on about Betty, Mam's sister, whose wedding Kev has invited her to in a fortnight.

Of course I haven't even thought about the wedding or who I'll take but Kar or Fee usually go to things like this with me.

'I can't,' Kar says when I ask her, 'Arnie's brother is

going away for a year and they're having a big send-off; he's insisting I go and meet all his family … sorry.'

'Ah come on, Kar, you can meet Arnie's family any time.'

'I promised and he says he's never felt like this before about anyone and he wants me to meet everyone!'

I roll my eyes. 'Ye're only going out a few weeks and you've known me for years!'

'I know. But I guess I have that effect on men.'

'You could take Ryan,' Fee interrupts.

'No can do,' Kar says, 'he and Dad are going to some big match next Saturday.'

The girls then go through every guy at school but there's no way I'm going to take any of them.

'Well that just leaves some of the girls,' Fee says, totally fed up with me. 'What about Katie?'

'She'll be working,' I say.

'Or Sue?' Kar asks.

'Maybe I don't need to take anyone,' I say.

'Of course you do,' Kar insists, 'or do you want to be a gooseberry all –'

Just then the doorbell goes again. Fee gets it and I nearly fall off the couch when she comes back in with Joey.

'Hey. I was on my way home from school and thought I'd see how you're doing,' she says.

'I'm fine.' I explain to the girls how Joey helped me the day before.

They don't seem to think anything of it and just start chatting about school and stuff and Fee makes tea and finds some chocolate biscuits and we actually end up having a pretty good laugh.

'So, are you doing anything next Saturday?' Kar asks as Joey stands to go.

I stare at Kar with my 'don't you dare say another word' eyes.

'Me?' Joey asks, 'Um, no, I've no plans; why?'

'Well, Flick's going to this wedding and she needs someone to go with her ... so, will you go?'

I swear I turn purple and can hardly breathe; if I survive I'm going to kill Kar.

'OK,' Joey says.

'Well then, it's sorted,' Kar says.

'If you're sure?' Joey says, looking at me.

'Yeah,' I croak.

Fee makes all the arrangements and I sit there totally tongue-tied, my mind a whirl.

'What the hell did you do that for?' I ask Kar the minute Joey's gone.

'Well you weren't going to ask her and she's nice and I can't go and you've absolutely *no one* else and you don't want to be a gooseberry with Kev and Fee all night – you'd be driven demented – so problem sorted!'

It seems to take for ever for the following Saturday and the wedding to come around and when it does I'm sick with nerves. I barely touch my breakfast and then feel doubly rotten because I haven't eaten. To top it all off I hop around town from the hairdressers to the beauticians with Mam and then take ages to dress, nearly making us all late for the wedding! It means that Joey gets the quickest of introductions to the folks. Mam doesn't even seem to recognise her and instead she and Dad just presume that Joey is Kev's new girlfriend and that I've brought Fee, which suits both Kev and me fine.

Everything is going great until Fee decides that she's going to find men for Joey and me. She drives me so mad that by the time the meal is over I'm ready to strangle her. Instead I make a quick getaway on my crutches out to the patio and the garden beyond. The second I hear the noise behind me I spin round; Joey is standing there with two glasses in her hand. She smiles as she hands me one.

'I thought you might need this.'

'Defo,' I say, taking a drink. 'Can you bloody well believe Fee? I swear I'm going to kill her tomorrow.'

'Come on,' she says, taking my already nearly empty glass, 'there's a bench over here; you can hide out for a while at least.'

I'm still ranting as I follow Joey down a short footpath and into a small enclosed garden. It's only then that I shut up.

There's a lighted water fountain in front of us with beds of red roses surrounding it. Joey sits down on a bench. I just stand there. Everything is so quiet and serious and I wish I was back among the crowds.

'Aren't you going to sit down?' she asks.

'Sure,' I say and I sit inches away from her. I can't think of a thing to say. My heart is beating so fast I can hardly breathe. I sneak a peak at her and right at that second she looks at me and it's like she knows what I'm thinking before I turn my face away.

'Maybe we should go back,' I say.

'We just got here, Flick,' she says really quietly.

'I know but –' I stop myself, knowing she'll be insulted if I insist.

'I've really had a lovely time,' she says.

'Even with Fee trying to set you up all day?' I try to lighten the mood.

'Seriously,' she says, 'thanks for inviting me.'

I give a faint smile. 'I, ah, had a great time too.'

'Flick,' she says after a minute. I swear my heart is going to explode. I can't seem to breathe or talk or anything. 'You know I really like you,' she whispers.

'I like you too,' I say quietly, staring at the ground; 'you're a good friend.'

'No,' she persists, 'I mean I really, *really* like you. I uh … I don't want to freak you out or anything but sometimes from the way you look at me I think you like me that way too.'

Even though they are words that I have dreamed of for so long I cringe when I hear them and for the hundredth time check to make sure there's no one around.

'I'm sorry if I've put you on the spot, but I couldn't go on much longer without telling you.'

I stare at her dress, afraid to meet her eyes. My throat has completely closed and I feel paralysed. She waits and when there's no reply she apologises again.

'I'm sorry Flick; I hope I haven't ruined things,' she says.

I look at her.

'I like you, too.' I say it so quietly that I'm not sure she's heard and for a second I'm relieved. Suddenly she gives a little laugh and grabs my hand.

'Really?' she asks. I'm too scared to reply. All I want to do is run away. I wish I hadn't said anything. She slides closer to me.

'Joey,' I whisper. She stops and stares at me. 'I … I …' I take a deep breath. 'I'm scared, I've never said anything like this to a girl before.'

'It's OK.'

'I don't think it is. I'm not like you – I wish I was but I'm not,' I say, trying to keep my voice as quiet as possible.

'Look, I know how you feel,' she whispers, giving my hand a tight squeeze.

'How could you?' I ask, unconvinced.

'Because I wasn't always this confident and sure of myself,' she replies. 'I'm nervous as hell sitting here beside you. But I always have to say how I feel, otherwise it just eats me up inside.' She looks at me for a few seconds. 'You're beautiful,' she whispers. I look away, my head reeling and my heart feeling like it's about to break. I look up and for a second we just stare at one another in the darkness and then, ever so slowly, she moves in towards me till I can feel her warm breath on my face. She pauses a second longer and as I close my eyes and hold my breath, our lips touch softly. My heart flips and for a brief moment I'm in heaven. Until a sudden noise brings me back to earth.

'Jeez, what was that?' I say, jumping up on my good leg.

'What?' she asks in a high, surprised voice, peering around.

'That rustling or crackling – didn't you hear it? It came from over there somewhere.'

'There's nothing there,' she insists.

'Listen, there it is again,' I whisper.

'It's probably just a bird,' she says.

'At this hour?' I hiss.

'Well, just a rat or mouse or hedgehog then,' she says, exasperated. 'Can't you just sit down?'

'Ugh, a rat, could there be one there?' A shiver runs up my spine.

'Sit down,' she says again.

'Ssh, just listen,' I say.

'What now?' she asks.

'I hear mumblings,' I whisper. 'Stop talking so loudly or they'll hear us.'

She leans back against the bench in the darkness, her face completely hidden in the shadows as I look around the empty garden.

'Maybe we should get back,' I whisper. 'We've been gone a while; they'll be wondering ...' She doesn't answer. 'Joey?'

I hear a sigh before she stands and for a moment I feel a pang of guilt but I ignore it and grab my crutches. I walk as quickly as I can back out onto the large open lawn then stand and wait for her. She's by my side in seconds.

'Gosh, I was so sure there was someone there,' I say as I look around.

'There wasn't,' she murmurs.

I begin to hobble on, afraid she'll suggest we return to where we were. We walk in silence for a few seconds, both watching the crowd laughing and talking on the patio.

'I'm glad we talked,' she says.

'Me too,' I lie.

She stops. 'Flick,' she says.

Reluctantly I stop and turn, conscious that if anyone was to look out onto the garden they'd see us standing there alone. 'I can wait,' she whispers.

I look down, embarrassed, before giving her a quick smile.

'Thanks,' I say.

She stays standing there, looking at me expectantly, but I can't say anything else. After a few seconds we walk on up the path in silence. I'm dying to be back inside, back where I can be seen. As we get closer to the patio I realise that there's no one out searching for me or watching or wondering what we're doing.

'Come on,' she says, 'lets get a drink. I'm buying.'

CHAPTER 41

'Flick! Flick, over here!'

It's Fee. I want to ignore her but I can't so, reluctantly, I turn in her direction. She's sitting talking to some guy.

'Simon, this is Felicity, better known as Flick; Flick, this is Simon.'

'Hi,' I say.

'Hey. Fee was telling me loads about you,' he says.

'All nice things, I promise,' she says. I give her one of my 'you're dead' looks, but I don't think she even notices.

'Simon's in sixth year in Cronan's and he's the winger for the senior team,' she announces.

'Oh, right,' I say, not really caring.

'I would have brought my CV,' he says, 'if I'd known you were going to go through my credentials like this.'

He and Fee laugh so I do too.

'OK, I gotta go find Kev,' Fee says. 'See you guys later.'

'No,' I blurt out, 'I mean, why not wait on Kev to come back here?' But she's already gone. 'Fee, I have to find Joey,' I call after her but she doesn't even turn around.

Simon knocks back the end of a pint while I silently curse Fee and wonder how the hell I'm going to escape.

'I didn't know you were here with someone,' he says. 'I'll let you go.'

For a second I say nothing; I really don't want to be stuck with him but I know what he'll think if he sees Joey.

'Oh, she's my friend … she's here with me.'

'Oh, "she"? I thought, when you said Joey …' he says.

'She went to the bar; she's probably looking for me now … I really should go find her,' I explain.

'If she's any way near as pretty as you, she's probably being chatted up right now.' He smiles.

'I still better check,' I say, about to move.

'Hey,' he says grabbing my arm gently, 'you're not going to leave me here all on my own, are you?'

I try to pull away but he's persistent and insists on helping me find her. It takes ages but in the end I spot her sitting at a table near the corner of the bar, alone.

'Hey,' I say and make a face to warn her about Simon. 'I was looking for you.'

'Were you?' she asks, staring coldly at me and then at him.

He is oblivious to Joey and grabs one of my hands.

'I'm a great palm reader,' he says, turning my hand

over. He begins tracing the lines lightly with his finger-
tips while I bite my lip and say nothing. He's in the middle of telling me that I'll have three children and a
wonderfully funny, dark-haired husband who, coinci-
dentally, will also be called Simon, when Kev and Fee
walk over. I pull my hand away and grab my glass only
for him to drape his arm across my shoulders. The next
hour is pure torture and I'm so relieved when he finally
goes to the bar for a round. He isn't gone long when
Mam and Dad appear to tell us they're heading home.

'I'm gonna go too,' Joey says.

I can see Mam and Dad looking at Kev, wondering
if there's been a bust up.

'Me too,' I say.

Fee and Kev stare disbelievingly at me.

'What about Simon?' Fee hisses.

'Just tell him I had to go,' I say.

'Do you want to come too, Fee?' Mam asks.

'Um, no, I might stay on for a little while longer,'
she says.

'Are you sure?' Mam replies in a surprised voice.

'I'm sure,' she says without explaining further.

'Well, how will you get home?' Mam persists.

'She can come with some of us,' Kev says in an off-
hand sort of way. Mam doesn't seem too happy with
the situation but says nothing more about it.

We climb into a taxi and head for home. Dad sits in

the front, directing the driver who doesn't need any directing, while I sit between Mam and Joey. With every bump and turn of the taxi I feel her beside me and know that in a few minutes she'll be gone. In the darkness I slide my hand onto the seat beside her. I wait for a few seconds then, holding my breath, I move it closer to her. Our hands barely touch before she pulls hers away and grabs her bag.

'Thanks a lot,' she says to no one in particular the moment the taxi pulls up by her house. 'I had a really lovely day.'

'I'm sorry,' I whisper as she opens the door and slides away from me. It's as if she doesn't hear. She bangs it closed and quickly walks away.

CHAPTER 42

Mam's dying to hear all the scandal when she comes up with breakfast the following morning. 'I really don't know anything about Kev or what he gets up to,' I lie, 'so please stop asking.'

'Well, what about Simon?' she persists. 'I saw you two having a great chat!' I make a face. 'Betty was telling me he's Brian's nephew and he's already been offered a sports scholarship for one of the big colleges.'

'You see, you know more than I do,' I say.

'Oh, be like that,' she says, her face lit up. Then she turns on her heel and leaves the room.

I lie back on my pillow and think about Joey. Actually, I've been thinking about her all morning. I know I have to ring her, I *have* to explain, but I'm dreading it. It takes me practically half the day to psych myself up and when I eventually dial her number I cross my fingers, hoping, like the coward that I am, that she doesn't answer. She does. 'It's Flick,' I say.

'Hi' she says.

'I, uh ...' Already I'm stuck for words and can't think of a thing to say.

'I just wanted to say thanks for coming yesterday.'

She doesn't reply. 'And I'm, uh, sorry about that Simon guy; he was an idiot and I, uh, I just couldn't get rid of him.'

There's silence on the other end of the phone so I waffle on, trying to convince us both that he was the one at fault. Joey remains tight-lipped.

'It was probably partly my fault that he stayed around,' I finally admit, desperate for her to say something. 'I'm sorry.'

'I don't know why you didn't tell him to go to hell,' she says.

'I know; I should have. It was stupid of me. It's just Fee was delighted that she had set us up and he was Brian's nephew and I guess I just didn't want to cause a scene. I know he was painful but I thought he'd get fed up and just go away if I kept ignoring him.'

'But you let him hold your hand and put his arm around you. That's not ignoring someone – that's letting them do what they want.' I wince at her words, and an image of Mike flashes into my mind. There's a lump in my throat and I clench my jaw to stop the tears.

'I'm sorry,' I say and try to explain again but she argues and disagrees. 'I just didn't know how to get rid of him,' I finally say. 'I really didn't mean to hurt you. I'm sorry.'

There's a short silence.

'OK,' she says.

I'm about to breathe a sigh of relief when she asks about us.

'Us?' I ask.

'Well, I know we talked a bit last night and I know you need time to work through some stuff but I really don't want to be messed around so if you're not interested please tell me now and I won't bother you any more.'

'No, I am, I am,' I say weakly.

'You're sure?' she asks.

'Yeah, of course,' I say in a slightly more convincing voice.

Her mood changes and suddenly she's on a high, planning all the things we could do. I try to explain that I need to take things slowly but I'm not sure she's listening any more. By the time I hang up I feel worse than ever and for the rest of the day my head spins through our conversation again and again.

That night I toss and turn imagining being out with Joey and being caught by someone or other. It's not pretty. Worse still, I hear her over and over saying that I let Simon do things to me, like I let Mike do things to me. Everything that I'd talked to Dr Rodge about, that I thought I'd closed the lid on, comes tumbling back out and starts rattling around my head and the nightmares that I thought were a thing of the past come right back with them.

CHAPTER 43

I don't say anything to Dr Rodge about the nightmares, which are getting worse and worse – I figure I can handle things myself.

On Tuesday, I invite Joey over after school, just to reassure her that I do like her. I'm nervous and excited all at the same time so I talk and talk and talk about everything and nothing. Before I know it, it's nearly five which means Mam's on her way home from work and I know I'll need to get rid of Joey fast or I'll have loads of explaining to do. She seems to sense there's something wrong and before I can even think of a good excuse she's telling me she has to go. I can tell she's annoyed but I'm just relieved and pretend nothing's up. She calls to the house a few times over the next couple of weeks. I wonder if people have started to notice her coming? Most days we just watch the TV and chat and eat and it's cool having her there but I know she wants to kiss me and I really want to kiss her but I'm too afraid. What if Mam arrived home? Or some of the girls called in? So I continue to ignore the fact that she's getting more and more fed up.

When she rings the following Saturday she's in foul humour. 'I just want to do something different,' she says, 'like go to the cinema or something like that.'

My stomach lurches. There's absolutely no way in high heaven I can be seen out with Joey.

'Yeah, but the exams are starting the week after next; Mam and Dad won't let me outside the door until they're over.'

'So are mine, but surely they'll let you have a break for an hour or two?'

We argue about it for ages until she eventually hangs up on me.

Damn it, I think, lying on my bed, trying to figure out a way around it. Finally I ring her and hope she'll agree to my plan.

She does.

CHAPTER 44

We meet outside the cinema at twelve on Monday. We've both dodged school and study classes. I'm really hoping this will pacify Joey and odds are there'll be no-one here at this time, so no-one will ever know. Just in case, I pick the worst film and buy the tickets while Joey's getting some grub. Five minutes later we're sitting at the back of a totally empty cinema. She is *so* not impressed that she has to sit through two hours of a horror film.

'I'm sorry,' I say, 'but we're here now; we might as well stay.'

'It's just I hate horror,' she says; 'it freaks me out.'

'It's about to start,' I say, without mentioning that it freaks me out too.

Just as the film is beginning, the doors open. I catch my breath as some old guy saunters in and ambles down towards the screen.

'Damn, he frightened the life out of me,' I whisper.

Joey sniggers. 'Serves you right,' she says.

Suddenly there's complete darkness in the cinema.

GERALDINE MEADE

'What the hell?'

A loud roar breaks the silence.

'Jesus,' I shout, grabbing her arm.

'Flick, you've just cut off my circulation,' she says, 'and aren't I the one who's supposed to be scared? I thought you liked horror?'

'I do,' I say as I sit back and try to relax.

I'm conscious of her beside me in the darkness, her arm inches from mine. I grab another large handful of popcorn and begin to munch, just to keep my mind off her. On screen there are a lot of shadows and noises and nothing much else.

'I don't think I can watch,' I hiss.

'Absolutely nothing has happened yet.'

'I know, but it's about to!'

She laughs. 'Feel free to grab my arm at any time.'

After an hour the old man near the front, totally fed up with us, turns and asks us to 'stop yelping'. But our nerves are shot to pieces and although we try to stop screaming it's impossible. The only difference now is that all our screeches are followed by a fit of the giggles. Joey grabs my hand.

'Run!' she shouts as the only human couple left on the planet are found by the demons. I scream, reacting to Joey rather than the film. Even when we've both calmed down she continues to hold my hand and I completely forget about the film. A scream from the screen and Joey grips my hand tighter, just for a second. All I want to do is kiss her, just once, and then I promise myself I'll never do it again. I'm so scared my heart is hammering and I can feel the blood pounding through my veins. I sit rigidly in my seat, afraid to move for fear of her letting go.

We're still holding hands when the film ends and the old man walks up the aisle muttering to himself. Neither of us says a word; we just stay staring straight ahead, watching the credits roll. My throat seems to have closed completely.

The names continue to roll and another song comes on and still we sit. Just one kiss, I think, here in the darkness where no one will ever see or know. She's looking at me. I give a nervous smile. I'm sure my heart will explode any minute. She moves a little towards me. I tilt my head and close my eyes. Our noses bump.

'Oh, sorry,' I say awkwardly.

She gives a quick smile as we lean towards one another again. Our lips touch but almost straight away I feel the armrest sticking into my ribs. I try to ignore it but I can't so I try to move subtly to avoid it. As I do, my foot slips and I kick her.

'Oh, sorry,' I say.

'Is everything OK?' she asks.

I explain about the armrest. She smiles and gently pushes me back in the chair as she moves to kiss me again. I feel her warm, moist lips on mine and I just freeze. I try to concentrate and do all the right things but I feel awkward and uncomfortable. She continues to press her lips against mine, willing me to respond. The minute I hear a noise at the door I jump a mile as does the guy that has come to clean up. He doesn't say anything, just stares at us. I turn away, pull up my hood and grab my crutches.

'We better get out of here,' I murmur. Without a word she grabs her bag, stands and walks out. As I watch her angry back walk away from me I quietly breathe a sigh of relief. The kiss was awful – a definite sign that I'm not a lezzer. We're just meant to be friends, I decide with relief as we head out into the sunshine. The moment we're outside I'm on guard again.

'So, I better head on,' I say quickly, 'what with my session and all that.'

She looks at her watch. 'It's only after two,' she says. 'Your session's not till four.'

'I know, but it'll take me for ever to walk with the crutches,' I say.

'Right, I'll see ya,' she says as she starts walking away.

'Joey, wait up,' I say. She stops and turns. When I reach her I don't know what to say. 'I, uh, I'm sorry that I have to go, and about the … you know,' I stutter.

'What?' she asks.

'You know … back in the cinema,' I mumble as an old woman walks past.

'You mean the kiss?' she asks.

I cringe. 'Yeah,' I say, 'but maybe it's for the best, don't you think?'

I see a flash of anger flicker across her face. 'That's it?' she says 'That's all you have to say?' She doesn't wait for me to reply. ' "Sorry, but it's for the best"?'

'I …' I begin, but I'm lost for words.

'I just can't believe you Flick! You're supposed to be my friend and yet you treat me like dirt.'

'I don't,' I say.

'Yes, you do,' she replies before I have time to defend myself. 'You know, I've finally figured you out. You're happy to have me around as long as there's no one about to see us together.'

'No, Joey, I swear that's not true,' I say.

'Isn't it? The other week at the wedding you let some guy drool all over you just so it looked good if people saw you with him. I've been going to your house when there's no-one there and having to leave before your Mum and Dad get home. And now this… I knew from the phone call you didn't want to be seen out with me and this just proves it: a crap film at midday in an empty cinema where no one will recognise you. Well, you might be happy doing that but I deserve better. I don't want to hide in the dark or whisper in corners or kiss when no one's watching. That's not enough for me. I want to be able to walk down the street holding hands and do whatever I want, when I want. I've always been straight up about who I am and I'm not going to change now ... no matter how mad I am about you.'

She stops and the million arguments that have been whirling around in my head disappear. I stand and stare.

'You'll never admit to yourself or anyone else that you like girls,' she continues angrily. 'You're so afraid of being different and having people realise that you're not the same as them that you'll do anything you can to conform. You want to sit in that tiny little box that's been made for you, no matter how cramped it is.' She takes in a deep breath. 'Inside you wouldn't even let yourself go, not even for a moment, to enjoy it. Then you tell me, so matter of factly, that it's for the best that it didn't work, like you even tried, or wanted it to. I'm tired of this. I'm tired of your games and I'm tired of pretending I'm something I'm not in front of your friends and family. I've told you how I feel; I thought you felt the same but I was wrong. There can't be any in-between, it's all or nothing. Otherwise it won't work.'

She stops and stares at me, waiting to hear words that never come. She lingers a moment longer. 'Bye Flick,' she says before she turns and walks away.

I stand and watch her go knowing that every word she said is true. She crosses the road and turns the corner without looking back.

'Bye,' I whisper before turning and limping the other way.

CHAPTER 45

I reach Dr Rodge's office at quarter past three and I sit flicking through magazines, trying not to think about Joey. By four I'm surer than ever that I'm not a lesbian; there's no way I'd feel so embarrassed and uncomfortable and awkward if I were. Dreaming about Joey and Becks is just a bad habit I've gotten myself into so I decide I'm just not going to do it any more. I tell myself it's like stopping smoking or giving up drink, sort of … Actually, it won't even be that bad cause I'll be able to kiss boys. By the time Dr Rodge calls my name I've it all figured out.

'Hello, Felicity,' she says. 'How are you today?'

'I'm good,' I say.

'So things are going well this week?'

'Yeah, pretty much,' I say.

She waits for a few seconds, obviously hoping that I'll elaborate.

'Well,' I say, 'I'm definitely not a, you know …'

She raises her eyebrows.

I take a deep breath. 'A lesbian,' I say.

'And when did you realise that?' she asks.

I'm not sure how to explain this to her and nor am I sure that I really want to.

'I just know,' I say.

She waits. She's so good at sitting through silences whereas I just want to throw words into these holes to fill them.

'I, uh,' I begin, then stop. 'I kissed another girl,' I blurt, 'just to check, and it wasn't right; it was awkward and weird. So that's how I know.' My eyes flick from their usual spot on the carpet to her face. Her expression doesn't change; she just nods.

'So did you want to kiss this girl or was it just to test out whether you liked kissing girls or not?' she probes.

I keep staring at the carpet remembering how, every minute I was with Joey, I wanted to kiss her.

'Maybe a little.'

'Sometimes things take practice,' she says. 'Maybe at the back of your mind you may not have wanted to enjoy this or you were scared or you needed to prove to yourself that this wouldn't work.'

'Well, it didn't. It's obvious I'm so not into girls.'

'Not even a little bit?' she asks.

'Nope,' I say, 'I was right, it was just a phase and it's over.'

'Trying to ignore any part of who we are isn't healthy, Felicity,' she says; 'it's damaging and it can really hurt us so you need to be sure that you're not changing just to suit other people.'

'Of course I'm not. Anyway, shouldn't you be helping me rather than confusing me with all this stuff? You're not helping, you know. You should be supporting me; you should be showing me how I can get through this stupid phase, not making it worse.'

'Science has proven, Felicity, that our sexual orientation is part of our genetic make-up; it's part of who we are and it doesn't change. Trying to be someone you're not is –'

'That's not true,' I say, standing up. 'Don't try telling me who I am, cause you don't know. I'm not one of those … I'm not like that! I never was and I never will be, so just leave me alone.'

I storm out the door, swearing I'll never come back and promising myself that it's the last time I'm ever going to think or talk about girls like that again.

CHAPTER 46

I don't show up for my appointment with Dr Rodge on Friday. I think I've gotten away with it till we're in the middle of dinner.

'You didn't go to Dr Rodgerie today?' Mam says as I push some pasta around the plate.

'I got held up at school so I missed it … I did try to ring but I couldn't get through.'

'Right,' she says sceptically, 'and when were you going to tell us?'

'Now,' I say. 'I was just about to say.'

She looks at Dad.

'So you're not thinking of leaving your sessions?' he asks.

'No,' I lie, 'although I'd prefer to go to a different counsellor.'

'But why?' Mam asks.

'Dr Rodge is so annoying and she never listens to what I say, ever, she just makes everything worse.'

'She's supposed to be one of the best,' Dad says.

'Well, you go to her, so,' I say, pushing back my chair. I storm out of the room.

I'm sitting on the bed, messing around on the guitar when Mam comes up later.

'Can I come in?' she asks, her head peeping round the door.

I don't think I have a choice in the matter so I don't say anything.

'Do you really want to find a new counsellor?' she asks as she sits down on the bed.

'Can't I just stop going to anyone?' I ask, 'it's been weeks and weeks and I'm better now.'

'I'm not sure,' she replies, 'Dr Rodgerie said you're making excellent progress and the sessions are helping a lot.'

I roll my eyes.

'It's just that if you go to someone new it will mean getting to know and trust them and starting from scratch all over again. Are you sure that's what you want?' she asks.

I imagine months of long, boring and painful sessions with someone worse than Dr Rodge.

'I'll just go back,' I finally say, but I'm silently promising myself that I'm going to do whatever it takes to finish with these blasted sessions as quickly as I can.

* * *

I head out with Kar and the girls from school on Saturday night while Fee and Kev are off having a romantic meal. Of course I drink loads, a) so I can forget about Joey and b) so I have the guts to snog someone. The 'someone' turns out to be this really sleazy geek who I last ten minutes with before heading to the loos and vomiting, but better that it's happened here than at home – at least that's what I tell myself as I stare into the toilet bowl. Kar and Arnie eventually get me into a taxi and bring me home to bed where I stay till three o' clock the next day. Mam and Dad are so not impressed.

I head back to my session on Monday; I swear it's the longest ever. After reassuring me for a bit Dr Rodge sits back and waits for me to do the talking. I hardly say anything and she says even less.

By the following Friday my brain is fried and things are rapidly going downhill but I still won't talk to Dr Rodge. I stand around outside for a few minutes after the session, then try to persuade myself as I walk away that I'm not bothered about Joey but I can't help looking back, just to make sure she's not there.

School's crap as well. The teachers have been on my back for weeks now, telling me that the exams are just around the corner, as if I need reminding. To top it all off I know for a fact that Mam and Dad are talking about me; they start whispering every time I leave the room and I know they're up to something. I'm wishing the tablets had worked that time and wonder if there's any other easy way for a coward like me to make it all stop.

CHAPTER 47

It's a dull and cloudy Saturday and I am standing by a grave in the freezing cold with Mam, Dad and Kev. I peer down into the darkness and a shiver goes up my spine. Mam is bawling, even worse than when grandma died and Dad's trying to console her while Kev is just standing there in a daze or half-asleep or something. I guess I must look much the same as him cause I can't for the life of me remember who it is that's actually popped their clogs. I look up and see Fee and Kar sniffling away as well. I try to catch their attention with a cough and then a sneeze but they don't seem to notice so I look around some more. Jeez, loads of people from school are here; maybe it's Moran or better still Cunningham that's bitten the bullet. But then the priest starts rabbiting on about how sweet and friendly and happy the poor sod was. Cunningham? Sweet? No way. I think,

'Kev,' I hiss. He doesn't hear me. 'Kev,' I say a little louder as I give him a dig, 'are you deaf?' There's absolutely no reaction.

'And so as we commit Felicity to the ground …' the priest drones.

I stop and stare, confused, then give a short laugh but no one even notices. I strain to see the small gold plate on the coffin and sure enough, there's my name.

'Wait,' I shout, 'that's not me; I'm here, look!' But he just keeps talking and these four big guys come and start lowering in the coffin.

'Wait, stop!' I shout. 'I'm right here; are you blind?'

They keep going.

'Mam, Mam, look, it's me! Mam, look at me!' I roar, but she just cries even harder and stares into the hole. I feel all sick and queasy and desperate.

'Dad,' I shout, 'Dad, will you just look at me?'

I'm just about to shake him when I slip and fall backwards. I scream before I land with a thud on top of the coffin. In seconds I'm standing, trying to claw my way back out of the narrow black hole but the sides are so steep and high and everyone seems so far away.

'Dad! Dad, please!'

I try the others when he doesn't respond.

'Kev, Mam, help me up; I've slipped in.' I shout over and over but they just stand there staring without seeing me.

'Someone, anyone, help, please, I'm here, I'm alive!'

Mam bends over and looks down at me.

'Oh Mam, thank God; I was so afraid.'

She throws something and I cover my face as pieces

of clay fall on top of me. Dad and Kev follow suit. My pleads turn to shouts of anger. I keep trying to climb out and, once, I nearly make it. Come on, I think, I'm nearly there. But at the last second I slip and fall right back down again. Just as the prayers finish the first drops of rain begin to fall. Immediately people turn and head for cover.

'Wait,' I shout as they turn away. But no one looks or hears or helps. 'Wait, please Mam, I'm sorry,' I shout as she walks away. I fall to my knees. 'Mam, Dad, I'm really sorry, please help me,' I cry. But there's no one there any more; they've all gone.

For a moment I stand looking up, wondering desperately what to do. Then she appears at the edge of the grave. She's all in black and she looks so sad and lonely and I'm so thrilled to see her.

'Joey,' I say and I see her head move a little, 'help me please, I can't get out.'

'It didn't have to be this way,' she whispers. 'It could have been different, better.'

'I know that now. I'm sorry; I just didn't know what else to do,' I reply.

She doesn't say anything, just stares down at me.

'I love you,' she whispers, 'and I always will.'

She throws a red rose towards me, a speck of color in my darkness. A tear falls down her face before she turns and walks away.

'Joey, wait,' I call but she doesn't look back. 'Joey, I'm

sorry, please wait, help me, I'm afraid, please, I'm sorry.'

But she's gone.

'Mam,' I scream, 'help me, help!'

I start to climb again, frantically, but I just can't get up. I stare up at the black clouds overhead. Everything is so dark and I'm so scared. I call again just as the first shovelful of clay is thrown on top of me, then another and another. I begin to scream as bit by bit I'm drowned in a sea of heavy blackness.

When my voice and all hope is gone I feel her in the darkness beside me, whispering and crying and telling me not to worry, that I'm safe, that she's here and everything will be OK. I close my eyes, exhausted.

CHAPTER 48

I wake slowly from the nightmare, still surrounded by darkness. Where am I? Am I dead? I wonder, my mind reeling. My eyes become accustomed to the dark and I'm relieved to see outlines of the old familiar things I've lived with for so long. I turn and look at the empty space beside me and wonder whether Mam had ever been there at all. I sit up, already afraid of going back to sleep, so I grab my dressing gown and a blanket and tiptoe downstairs to the sitting-room. I stop in the doorway. Mam and Dad are there. Dad's holding Mam, trying to comfort her. She's crying. I want to run the other way, to slide back unseen into the darkness and back to my room but the moment I take a step backwards a floorboard creaks and they both look up.

'Felicity,' Dad says with a smile as Mam quickly dries her eyes, 'are you OK?'

'Yeah.'

'We thought you'd fallen back asleep. Come and sit and I'll make us all some nice hot chocolate.' Dad suggests.

I do as I'm told. 'Is everything all right, Mam?' I ask, not really wanting to hear the answer.

'Yeah, yeah,' she replies, giving me a brief smile of reassurance. 'So, how are you?' she asks.

'Fine,' I lie.

'Do you remember the nightmare?' she asks. I shake my head, hoping she'll give up. 'It's just … you were calling out a lot … for me … and Dad and I just wondered …' She trails off.

'Sorry,' I mumble.

'I'm worried about you, Felicity,' she whispers and she's wringing her hands.

'I'm fine,' I reply weakly.

'No, you're not,' she says shaking her head. 'I know you keep saying you are, but you're not eating, you're not sleeping, you seem so sad all the time and it scares me.'

'It's just a teenage thing,' I say, trying to laugh it off.

'I just don't know what to do.' she says. 'I don't know how to help.' She folds her arms in tightly to her chest and sits for a moment with her head down while I sit quietly watching her, wishing I could escape. 'It was just so awful that day when we found you,' she murmurs, 'I didn't know what to do … I felt so helpless.'

Oh God no, I think, not this, please not this.

'And when I saw you being put into that ambulance, not moving … I didn't even think you were breathing …' she sniffs, then puts her head in her hands. 'I thought you were dead,' she whimpers and her words sound all distorted.

Tears are flooding down her face and although I lean forward a little I don't move off the couch. I just want Dad to be back beside her. I know I should reassure her and all that but I haven't a clue what to say. I feel a lump in my throat as I watch her.

'It was the worst moment of my life, seeing you like that, my baby, my little girl,' she says as she shakes her head, as if trying to forget the memory. 'It broke my heart,' she sobs. 'It's worse than an accident or an illness – at least you've no control over them … but *this* … I felt it was my fault. I hadn't seen the signs. I hadn't been looking at you or listening to you closely enough. I let it happen.'

She sobs uncontrollably and I automatically move towards her chair and place my hand on her back.

'It wasn't your fault Mam; it was just me,' I say, feeling a tight pain across my chest. 'Please don't cry … it wasn't your fault, I swear.'

But she just keeps crying, ignoring my half-hearted attempts to reassure her.

'I can see it all starting again, Felicity, and I'm so scared. I don't want you to feel like this. I don't want you to think that you've no other choice but nothing I do seems to get through.' She starts crying again. I want to tell her to 'shhh' but I don't; I don't do anything, just stand there. 'I just don't know what to do…whenever I ask you if you're all right you just tell me you're fine. But you're not; I know you're not. Those signs that I missed the first time are back again. I can see it on your face; I can hear it in all the things you don't say. I can *feel* it.'

She looks up at me and I look away. Tears prick my eyes and I quickly blink them back before they escape.

'I can't let it happen again, Felicity,' she says, wiping the back of her hand across her eyes. 'I *won't* let it happen again.' I bite my lip, feel the metallic taste of my own blood and say nothing. 'If I can't help you then I'm going to get someone who will,' she continues a little more adamantly.

I think of Dr Rodge.

'I'm going to ring Dr Rodgerie in the morning about taking you back to hospital for a while,' she says.

'What?' I say, my voice suddenly rising. 'Are you serious?'

She looks up at me and nods.

'Please, Mam, don't,' I cry. 'I'm doing really well with Dr Rodge, really I am; I like her, I swear.'

'Felicity, I'll do anything to stop this happening again. They'll know what to do and how to help. They do it all the time.'

'Please, don't put me back inside,' I beg.

'They said if you ever needed to go back, even for a day or two, that you could,' she continues, 'and maybe you'll talk to them.'

'I won't, I swear, I won't tell them anything,' I say, tears streaming down my face.

'I have to,' she says.

'Please, Mam,' I whisper.

'Then tell me what's wrong Felicity,' she sobs. 'I can help.'

I shake my head. 'It's nothing; there's nothing wrong.'

'Please, Felicity … is it something to do with me or Dad? Maybe it's school and exams?' I continue to shake my head. 'Is it a boy? We've all had boy trouble,' she says, a little hysterical now. 'Felicity, if you can't tell me then I've no other choice. Please …' She pauses. 'Are you being bullied?'

'No, it's nothing like that,' I reply, feeling trapped from her constant questions. I move away from her and sit down on the sofa. I try to think but she won't stop talking and asking questions.

'Why won't you talk to me, Felicity?' she asks pleadingly.

'Because you'll hate me,' I whimper.

I hang my head, letting the tears flow. After a moment I feel her sitting beside me and putting her arm around me.

'Tell me,' she whispers.

But I can't say anything.

'Is it drugs?' she asks.

I shake my head and hear her breathe a sigh of relief.

'Are you pregnant?'

'No.'

She sits quietly for a moment. 'Whatever it is, it's going to be OK' she promises.

'It's a girl,' I blubber.

'A girl?' Mam asks, confused. 'Who? What's happened?'

'It's Joey, the girl from counselling,' I continue.

'Joey?' Mam repeats. 'I don't understand; have you two had a row?'

'Sort of,' I say. I can see her face brightening already.

'But we can fix this,' she says. 'What did you fight about?' She waits, trying to read my face before I even say the words.

'Us,' I murmur.

She gives me a puzzled look. My heart is racing. I don't want to say any more. I don't know how to say any more. I close my eyes.

'We're in love,' I whisper.

'With the same boy?' she asks, still confused.

I take a deep breath and look quickly at her, then look away.

'No,' I whisper, 'with each other.'

'What?' she asks, then stops as what I've said sinks in. I watch her shocked face until I can't bear it any longer, then I hang my head again. 'You and Joey?' she says, 'are in love? Like boyfriend and girlfriend?' Her voice wavers.

'No,' I say looking up, 'like girlfriend and girlfriend.'

She sits in stunned silence. 'Don't you like boys?' she asks quietly.

'No.'

'But … but what about that boy from school and Kevin's friend Mike and Simon?'

A shiver runs up my spine and I shake my head. I knew she wouldn't understand; I knew it wouldn't help. I start to cry.

'Felicity, it's all right,' she says, 'we all go through these phases.'

'It's not a phase,' I say. 'I've always liked girls.'

'Are you sure?'

I nod my head.

'But how do you know?'

I shrug. 'I just do.'

'Well, that's OK.' She falters. 'What about Joey?'

'Joey told her family years ago. She's told all her friends too.'

'I see,' Mam says. 'So, how long have you two been together?' she ventures.

'We haven't… I don't *want* to be a … a … like that. I didn't want anyone to know so we never did anything. Are you disgusted?' I ask.

'No, of course not,' she says. She sits in silence for a moment. 'I'm glad you told me. I don't want you to keep things bottled up. I want you to be able to come to me and tell me things. I can help.'

We sit for a while longer. Mam keeps telling me that everything is going to be OK but she doesn't sound too convincing. Dad doesn't arrive back with the hot chocolate and eventually, just before six, Mam suggests I go back to bed for a rest. I nod but don't move.

'Are you going to ring the hospital this morning?' I ask.

She shakes her head. 'I don't think there's any need, for the moment, now you've told me what the problem is. I think we can sort this out ourselves. Now, off you go,' she says again, giving me a quick hug.

Seconds after I've left the room, I hear Dad return.

'Well?' he asks.

'I think we need something stronger than chocolate,' I hear her say.

I head upstairs and collapse into bed, wondering whether I've done the right thing telling her. For some reason I'm not so sure that I have.

CHAPTER 49

I can't sleep and after a while I creep out and sit on the landing. Mam and Dad are still talking downstairs and I have to strain my ears to hear them; I just manage to make out their conversation.

'I just can't believe it,' Dad says. 'Who ever would have thought?'

'I know,' Mam agrees, 'it's terrible; why Felicity? Why can't it be someone else? Someone else's daughter? Why does it have to happen to us?'

There's a few seconds' silence and I know she's crying.

'Can you imagine what everyone's going to say? I can just see them now ... Oh, Jack, what on earth are we going to do?'

'Do?' Dad snaps. 'Do? Your daughter has just come to you after probably years of torment to tell you her greatest secret and you're going on like there's something wrong with her! And worrying about what everyone else will *say*? And what we'll do to *fix* her?'

There's silence.

'So I'll tell you what we're going to do, Cathy: we're

going to support her and tell her that it's fine to be a lesbian and be with girls and as long as she's happy then we're happy. And we're not going to try to change her or fix her or sort her out or make her feel like the freak that she thinks she is.'

'Shhhh,' Mam interrupts, 'she'll hear you … I'm just worried – think about how she'll be treated in school and when she's out and about. Everyone will be looking and talking; I know what they're like.'

'Cathy,' he growls, 'who the hell cares about everyone else? We've got a second chance here; she's confided in us. Don't you know how difficult that must have been for her? So we are going to be happy for her and we are going to support her one hundred per cent, without question.' I hear him walking to the door. 'You're always so damn worried about having us appear to be perfect. Well, we're not and if you try to change her or make her feel in any way ashamed of who she is then I swear it's not just a daughter that you'll lose.'

I barely make it back inside before he pounds up the stairs.

I lie in bed all morning, dreading the thought of facing them. I knew she'd be disgusted; I knew it. I eventually drag myself out of bed after twelve. By the time I shower and dress another hour has gone by, an hour of wondering what I'll say to them, and worse still, what they'll say to me. I open the bedroom door and quietly make my way downstairs, then stand in the hallway psyching myself up. Eventually I take a deep breath, open the door and walk in.

'Hi.'

'Hi hon,' Mam says with a tight smile, 'how are you this morning?'

'This afternoon,' Dad corrects her, looking up from the paper.

'OK,' I say.

'Well, you're just in time for brunch. Will you set the table?' she asks.

She's got this voice on, like she's talking to a visitor or a stranger and not really to me.

'Yeah,' I say, but all I want to do is get out of here. 'Where's Kev?' I ask.

'He went out somewhere a while ago, God only knows where,' Dad says.

I'm so embarrassed being around them now and I wish I was anywhere but here. I set the table and Mam dishes up while I sit with my head down.

'Felicity,' Dad says before clearing his throat.

I look up, red-faced.

'I'm glad you and Mam had a good chat last night. I know it was difficult for you to tell her, but it was the right thing to do. We just want you to be happy, hon, and if liking girls makes you happy, then we're happy too.'

'OK' I croak, but I'm soooo embarrassed and just want him to stop talking.

'I have to say, I was a little shocked last night when

you told me,' Mam says, 'but it's not anything to be ashamed of.' Even though I know she's lying I nod.

'So, this girl, Joey,' Dad says, 'is she the same girl that Kev brought to the wedding?'

'Kev brought Fee to the wedding and, uh, Joey came as my friend,' I explain awkwardly.

'Oh,' Mam says.

'Why don't you bring her to dinner some evening? We'd love to meet her again,' Dad says.

Mam doesn't say anything.

'Well, we sort of had a row,' I say, 'so we're not really friends any more.'

He insists on me telling them the story and then insists even more that I go and sort it out.

'You think?' I ask looking from him to Mam.

'Yeah,' Dad says, 'you've been miserable without her. If you just tell her how you feel I bet ye'll sort it out in a jiffy.'

Mam gives a small smile and tries to look enthusiastic about the idea.

'What if she doesn't want to see me?' I ask.

'Trust me, she will,' he replies, 'but if she doesn't at least you'll have tried.'

I smile and quickly finish my grub, suddenly excited at the prospect of seeing her. Within minutes I'm heading out the door.

CHAPTER 50

Getting to Joey's gaff seems to take for ever and when I finally arrive I stand outside, scared to go any further. It takes all my nerve to walk up the drive and ring the doorbell. I wonder what she'll say when she sees me, how she'll react, and I pray she won't tell me to go to hell or slam the door in my face. I take a deep breath to try to stop myself panicking and I'm just wondering whether I should go when the door swings open. I stand open-mouthed, in shock because there in front of me is Dr Rodgerie. She stops and stares as well.

'Felicity, is everything OK?'

My head is in a whirl; there's only one reason why Dr Rodge is here.

'Has something happened? Is Joey OK?' I blurt out.

'Mum, have you seen my sneakers?' Joey hollers from upstairs.

'Oh my God,' I murmur, then I turn and nearly run down the driveway.

'Felicity,' she calls, but I don't turn round. Instead I race across the road and down towards the bus stop, willing one to come, but it's Joey I see running towards me when I look up.

'Flick,' she pants, 'please let me explain.'

'I can't believe she's your mother!' I say. 'Why the hell didn't you tell me?' I don't wait for her reply. 'I bet you were having a great laugh about me.'

'Flick, don't be crazy; it wasn't like that at all. I –'

'You accuse me of not admitting to things, of not being open and honest and all the time you were keeping this a secret?'

'It's not the same thing,' Joey argues, shaking her head.

'It's exactly the same thing,' I insist.

'I wanted to tell you, Flick, I swear. That first day you just presumed I was her patient and I didn't get a chance to explain that I wasn't.'

'So now it's my fault?'

'No, it's just that I never got the proper chance and then as time went on I thought you would probably quit the counselling sessions and I didn't want to ruin that for you and I thought that you'd run a mile from me when you found out.'

'Damn right,' I say.

'Look, I know I was being selfish but I thought that if we got to know one another then maybe … Then it just got more and more difficult to say it the more I got to know you.'

I stand in silence, my jaw clenched. I think of all of

the things I've told Dr Rodge, all the things she knows about me and I wonder whether Joey knows them too.

'Mum's going to kill me when I go back,' she murmurs.

'Good,' I say, but I'm secretly wondering why.

'I never told her I was meeting you or going to your house or the wedding,' she explains. 'I just pretended I was with my friends from school all the time. I knew she'd stop me straight away if she found out. She's always going on about ethics ... I'll probably be grounded for, like, ever.'

I stand rigidly against the wall, unwilling to hear her excuses but relieved that Dr Rodge didn't know about me either.

'I'm sorry,' she says again.

I don't reply. I look up the road the minute I hear the bus and then reluctantly look at her. She's as beautiful as ever and in those seconds I feel my resolve weaken a little.

'So you don't go to a shrink?' I say.

'No,' she replies quietly.

'And you've never been to one?'

She shakes her head. I clench my jaw, feeling the anger resurface. I feel like such a fool.

'Flick, I didn't mean to make you feel bad; I never wanted to hurt you,' she repeats. 'Anyway, there's nothing wrong with counselling; loads of people go and if it's any consolation I pretty much get counselling twenty-four seven from Mum, whether I like it or not.'

'It's not,' I say.

'I really am sorry. I never meant to lie to you; I like you too much for that,' she says as the bus pulls to a stop. 'Can't you stay and talk?' she pleads as I move towards it.

'You're joking, right? How the hell do you expect me to look at your Mam after everything that's happened?'

'Please,' she begs quietly, 'there's a small park around the corner. We could go there?'

I stand confused for just a moment. The bus driver is watching us impatiently.

'Don't mind me, love,' he says sarcastically in a gruff voice, 'I've got all day!'

'I can't,' I say to Joey and step onto the bus. I turn back towards her. 'I –' The doors slam shut as the bus jerks forward. I crane my neck and watch her standing there. A large cloud of black smoke belches from the exhaust as the bus accelerates on down the road, leaving Joey and all hope of us being together behind.

* * *

Dad's asleep in the armchair when I get in. I grab the controls and plop myself on the couch. The minute I flick onto another channel from the sports he wakes.

'What? What?' he asks groggily, rubbing his eyes and

trying to get his bearings. 'Felicity, what are you doing here?'

I'm about to say something but there's this tightness and I can't really breathe properly and I just know I'm gonna cry. He comes over and sits down on the couch beside me.

'Tell me what happened,' he says.

'It was a disaster,' I wail, crying again.

He hugs me close. 'What? What happened?' he asks again.

I tell him the story. Just as I'm finishing it Mam comes in and doesn't look a bit surprised to see me.

'That was Dr Rodgerie on the phone,' she says.

'What? What did she want?'

'She wanted to check that you're OK. I think she was as shocked to see you this afternoon as you were to see her,' Mam begins before telling us their whole conversation.

'So she definitely didn't know?'

Mam shakes her head.

'And you don't think she told Joey anything about me?'

'Absolutely not,' Mam replies adamantly. 'She's a professional; she has a code of ethics. She's not allowed to tell anyone, not even us. She rang because she's worried about you, Felicity, she doesn't want you to feel betrayed or upset. She wants you to understand that she knew nothing about any of this until you came to the door and Joey ran out after you. I did tell her that you had told us your … news last night. I hope you don't mind.'

I shake my head.

'She was delighted,' Mam continues, 'and she's very proud of you.'

I grimace in embarrassment.

'Anyway, she said that we could discuss you going to another counsellor, especially if you and Joey are going to be, uh, good friends,' she finishes.

'I won't be seeing Joey again,' I say.

'Now, Felicity, don't you think that's a little extreme?' Dad asks.

'No, I don't.'

'I know she should have told you,' Mam says, 'but I suppose she just didn't know how. Sometimes the longer you wait to admit something the more difficult it is to say. I'm sure she never meant to lie to you.'

'It just won't work,' I insist, shaking my head.

'Why not?' she asks.

I sniff back the tears, knowing she's relieved.

'Of course it would,' Dad insists.

I shake my head adamantly.

'What's wrong, Felicity?' Dad asks. He keeps asking me until I finally blurt it out.

'I'm scared.'

'Scared of what?' he asks, surprised.

'I'm scared of people finding out that I'm a lesbian. I'm scared of how they'll react and what they'll say and what they'll think of me. I'm scared they won't like me any more and they'll avoid me.'

Mam hugs me tightly. Dad sits quietly for a while.

'Flick,' he says at last. 'I'd love to tell you that everything will be fine, that people won't react badly or say hurtful things; some people probably will. But you can't let those few people and their narrow-mindedness stop you from living the life you want to lead. If you do you'll end up so unhappy and we just couldn't bear to see you like that.' He pauses. 'Just remember that the people who matter will love you as they always have, no matter what, and they will understand that this is a part of who you are.'

'Kev's going to be totally grossed out and so will Fee and Kar. And I'd say everyone at school will have such a laugh and say the most awful things,' I snivel.

'It doesn't matter what other people think,' Dad says.

'Of course it does. It matters to me.'

He sighs. 'You can't let what others say and think rule your life, and you can't just do things to please others. You're going to have to be strong and stand up for what you believe in and what you want.'

I nod but I'm not convinced.

'You'll be old news within a week of telling people,' he promises, glancing towards Mam, obviously looking for some support.

'It'll be OK,' she promises. 'It's all going to work out just fine.'

I make a face, knowing they're lying.

'So what are you going to do about Joey?' Dad asks.

'I dunno,' I say.

'I think you should talk to her and sort this out,' he says.

'OK,' I mumble.

'I also think you need to tell Kevin and maybe some of your friends soon,' he continues. 'You don't want to be sneaking around behind their backs.'

I cover my face with my hands. 'I just dread the thought of it.' I feel a shudder go up my spine.

'Well, the sooner you do, the better you'll feel,' he says.

'You're right,' I finally admit. 'And I will do it soon; I promise.'

I just never thought it would be as soon as he had planned.

CHAPTER 51

We're eating some pasta a while later when Kev barges in the door, his usual grin on his face.

'Any dinner left?' he asks, veering towards the cooker.

'Hi to you too, Kev,' Dad says.

'There's a little bit, if you want it,' Mam says.

'Great. I just have to grab a quick shower and change; can you heat it for me Mam? I'll be back down in a few minutes.' He goes pounding up the stairs without waiting for her reply.

'Cheeky monkey,' she complains as she puts on some fresh pasta and heats the sauce.

'You know, now would be a good time to tell him,' Dad says after a few minutes.

'No way,' I say. But he pushes and pushes until I give in.

Seconds later Kev thumps back down the stairs.

'Thanks.' He grabs the plate and a can from the fridge. He sits at the table opposite me, clean shaven and scrubbed from head to foot.

'So where are you and Fee off to tonight?' Dad asks.

Kev glares accusingly across the table at me.

'Felicity didn't tell us; we figured it out ourselves,' Dad says.

Kev shrugs. 'The Vault,' he answers between mouthfuls, 'The Realm are playing,' he says before stopping to devour most of his grub.

'Kev, you'll get indigestion; will you please slow down?' Mam says.

He pauses wordlessly, then, grabbing the can, he takes a long drink.

'Oh, for God's sake,' she grumbles, continuing to analyse his every move.

'You could come, too, if you want,' he says to me, 'and Joey, if you're worried about being a gooseberry!'

'No, thanks,' I murmur before looking at Dad, who nods encouragingly.

'Kev?' I falter.

'What?' he replies, scraping the bowl.

'There's something I wanted to tell you,' I say.

'So tell me,' he says.

I wait.

'What?' he asks.

'It's just that I'm … I just wanted you to know that I'm –'

'You're not pregnant, are you?' he says, looking from me to Mam.

'Of course not,' I snort.

'Well, that's OK, then,' he says, taking another drink.

'I'm a lesbian,' I suddenly blurt out.

He spews the mouthful of drink across the table. 'Fuck off!' He laughs.

'I'm being serious, Kev,' I say as I hear the quiver in my voice.

'What? No way; you're joking, right?' he says, staring at me. I shake my head. 'I don't believe it,' he says with another laugh.

'What's so funny?' Mam asks.

'Flick being a lezzer.' He shakes his head. 'Let me guess – you and Joey?' he says.

I just bite my lip.

'I should've known,' he says.

'So, is that all you've got to say?' Mam asks.

'She has good taste in women,' he says with a grin before he walks away.

'Where are you going?' she calls.

'Out,' he replies and with a bang of the door he's gone.

'That didn't go so badly,' Dad says.

'Yeah, right,' I say

'He treats this place like a hotel,' Mam complains, 'running in and out without a bit of manners.'

'Well, maybe it's time he got his own place,' Dad says, 'or we start charging him rent. He'll definitely appreciate you then.'

Within minutes the doorbell rings. 'I knew it,' Mam says, getting up. 'He's always forgetting something.'

'Sit down,' Dad orders, 'your dinner's going to be freezing. Flick, you're finished, get the door and tell him to take keys – I don't want to be getting up during the night to let him in.'

I head for the door, knowing he's going to have yet another smart-assed comment for me. 'So what did you forget this –' I stop and stare, 'Joey,' I say in a half-whisper, her name catching in my throat.

'Hi,' she says with a smile. 'Sorry to be showing up on your doorstep but I was wondering if we could talk.'

I automatically look back towards the kitchen to Mam and Dad who are chatting away.

'I could meet you somewhere else if you wanted?' she suggests.

'Uh, no,' I say, opening the door a little wider, 'come in.' My heart is pounding so hard when I close the door behind her.

'Well,' Mam calls, 'what did he forget?'

'Um, it wasn't Kev,' I say, coming into the kitchen, 'it's Joey.'

'Oh,' Mam says, 'Joey, come in. How are you?'

'Hi Joey,' Dad says with a grin, 'it's nice to see you again.'

'Would you like something to eat?' Mam asks, beginning to fuss. 'There's some lovely pasta or some –'

'No thanks,' she says, 'I ate before I came out, but thanks anyway.' She stands awkwardly, as do I beside her.

'Right, well, we're just on our way out,' Dad says, 'so we'll see you two later.'

'No, we're not,' Mam begins.

'Oh, yes, we are,' he insists as he stands, grabs his keys, wallet and Mam's hand before heading out the door.

We're standing in the kitchen, totally alone.

'I'm sorry about today,' she blurts out immediately. 'I felt so bad that I hadn't told you about Mum. I really didn't mean to keep it from you or for you to find out the way you did … I know it sounds pathetic but I thought you'd run a mile when you knew.' She pauses and gives a small smile. 'And you pretty much did.'

'I nearly got sick when I saw your Mam,' I begin.

'I know, I know,' she says, 'she killed me when you left earlier; she started going on about her profession-alism and how I had totally jeopardised your relation-ship.' We end up talking about it for ages, going around in circles and saying the same thing over and over again.

'I'm really sorry,' she says for the umpteenth time.

'I'm sorry too … about how I treated you that day outside the cinema; you were right to be angry,' I say before pausing.

'It wasn't fair for me to say those things,' she says, 'or to make you do something that you weren't ready to do.'

I shrug and for a minute I can't think of anything to say. 'I'm glad you came,' I say.

'I am too,' she says. 'So, are we cool?'

'Yeah,' I say, 'we're cool, but there's something I have to tell you.'

'Oh,' she replies. 'What? Tell me.'

But I don't say anything cause I know the minute it's out there's no going back.

'Please, Flick,' she says, 'I hate waiting.'

'Oh, really?' I say with a laugh.

Then she grabs both my wrists in her hands and pushes me back against the wall.

'Tell me,' she says, 'or I'll have to use force!'

I gasp then laugh at her determined face.

'Tell me!' she repeats, gripping my wrists tighter.

I keep laughing, nervous and excited.

'Flick,' she warns with a faint smile.

I eventually stop and say, 'I told Mam and Dad that we … that I … love you.'

'What? You did not!' she cries, amazed, looseining her grip. 'What did they say?'

'Dad's great; Mam's pretending to be cool about it but she's so not,' I say.

She shrieks.

'Shhh,' I say.

'But there's nobody here,' she says. She leans towards me. 'So, can we try this again?'

'What?' I ask nervously.

'This, for starters,' she whispers as her lips gently

touch mine. She pulls her head away slightly, gauging my reaction.

I open my eyes. 'I think I need a bit more practice.'

'No problem.' She laughs.

CHAPTER 52

It turns out to be one of the longest and most stressful weeks in the history of my life. On top of all of the exam stress Mam nags me every evening to ring Dr Rodge.

'You missed your session on Monday and you'll just have to go and face her at the clinic tomorrow unless you call her,' she says.

'I'm not going back,' I say. 'I'd be mortified, what with Joey and everything.'

'Then tell her,' she says, handing me the number.

'Can't you?' I ask.

'Ring her,' she orders.

I make a face and dial the number, hoping she won't answer but of course she does. I stumble through the conversation, hating every second of it. She tells me how I've made such great progress by talking to Mam and Dad but suggests I go to this other counsellor for a while. She even invites me for dinner when the exams are over.

'Oh, sure,' I say but I have no intention of going.

Mam wants me to ring the other counsellor straight away.

'I've too much study; I'll ring her next week,' I holler as I pound upstairs.

I've planned to study for the evening just so I'm not blankly staring at another exam page. So I can't believe it when I wake up some time after nine to my phone ringing. It's Joey and we chat for ages but then she starts planning stuff for the weekend.

'I really can't go out. I've too much study, Joey; I'm sure you have, too.'

'Ah, come on, we've only got a few next week,' she says. 'Anyway, we need a break and I'm sure your parents won't mind.'

We argue for ages; I really don't want anyone to see us. I haven't even told Kar and Fee yet and I just couldn't bear all the leering and smart remarks from the lads but Joey doesn't seem to understand.

'Tell them tomorrow,' she says, 'and who the hell cares about the guys anyway?'

In the end I tell her I have to go and study. I hang up. How the hell am I ever going to tell the girls?'

Needless to say, Friday is another disaster. I leave the exam half an hour early and sit waiting for Kar and Fee in the locker room. Even after psyching myself up I can't bring myself to tell them my news so instead they just talk about Arnie and Kev and their plans for the weekend while I listen and say nothing, knowing Joey isn't going to be impressed. That's why I don't ring her when I get in and still haven't called her by dinner-time. So I'm totally shocked when the doorbell rings in the middle of dinner and Dad comes back with Joey behind him.

'Oh, hi,' I say. 'What are you doing here?'

'I've a surprise,' she says, 'two tickets for The Script!'

I stare at her.

'They're playing in town; Mum let me use her credit card earlier to book them,' she laughs excitedly. 'I thought it might get your mind off the study for a while.'

'That's really thoughtful of you, Joey. Isn't it, Felicity?' Dad asks.

'Yeah, it's great,' I lie, knowing there are definitely going to be loads of people from school there.

'Why don't I give you two a lift?' he suggests.

'Sure,' I say unenthusiastically, 'just gimme a few minutes.'

Joey and Dad chat all the way there. I try to join in but can't; I'm bricking it. Sure enough there are gangs everywhere when Dad stops the car so with my head down I follow Joey towards the entrance.

'Flick! Hey, Flick, over here!' someone calls.

'Hey, Costello, the queue's this way,' one of the lads shouts.

I look over to see Sue and Amanda from my class waving excitedly at me.

'I'll just be a minute,' I say to Joey.

'I'll come with you,' she says.

'No,' I say in alarm.

She's not impressed.

'It's not you,' I explain quickly, 'it's them; they're, well, they're just so immature. I'll meet you at the door.'

I walk away before she has time to argue.

'Hey,' I say, heading towards the girls.

'Hey,' they reply in unison.

'Who's that?' Sue asks, nodding towards Joey.

'Oh, just a friend,' I say.

'What friend?' Amanda asks.

'I mean … my cousin. She arrived at our gaff this

evening and she has tickets to the gig. It's such a pain – I don't even like her,' I blurt out, 'but I couldn't pass this up.' I don't know why I keep talking but I do. I hate myself.

'Well, hold on for us; we're hoping to get some too and then we can all go together; it won't be so bad,' Sue suggests.

'OK,' I agree lamely, having no intention of it. 'I better go find her; I'll wait just inside.'

'Cool,' they agree. I turn and walk back to the large glass doors. Joey's waiting and she doesn't look happy.

The night turns out to be a complete disaster. Joey keeps trying to hold my hand and whisper things in my ear and all I want to do is run a mile. I barely even get to see the band cause I'm looking around so much, making sure that no one I know is watching. Thankfully the venue's so big that I don't get to meet any of the gang again and we even manage to escape a few minutes early so I don't bump into anyone. I walk down the road quickly with Joey following behind.

'What was all that about?' she asks.

'All what?' I ask

'Hiding in the corner and treating me that way and running out before it was even over?'

'Not here,' I hiss, looking towards the arcades across the road before I turn and walk on.

'Oh for God's sake, Flick,' she says as she stares after me, 'nobody cares.'

We head back to my gaff, both angry.

'I'm home,' I shout as we come in the door.

There's no reply, just complete silence. I check the house – there's no one home. My mood has suddenly lifted!

'I just don't know why you were acting like that,' Joey begins as we head into the sitting-room.

'Oh, shut up,' I say with a grin as I shove her onto the couch and fall on top of her. We begin to kiss – the band, the worry, already forgotten. It turns out to be the best night of my life, ever!

CHAPTER 54

I race into school on Monday morning, dead late. Damn, I think as I run towards the door, they've all gone in. I pull it open as quietly as I can but even at that all heads turn and stare. I dodge between a few tables before quickly sliding into my seat. By eleven I'm exhausted. I have to get out of here, I think, as Rino, our accounting teacher, walks past me. I know he'll be livid when he sees me go, but I figure it's an extra half hour that I can study for business, my final exam, after lunch.

All eyes are on me yet again but I don't look round, just clench my jaw and plaster an 'I don't give a hoot' smile on my face. I start to breathe again the minute I'm outside the door and, grabbing my bag, I sneak off to find a quiet corner. I start off well and fly through two or three chapters – that's until my phone starts beeping. First Fee then Kar starts texting, wondering where I am. Fat chance, I think as I switch the phone to silent and get back to my book. My eyes flick open the minute the door does. I look around dazed wondering where the hell I am.

'Jeez, Flick, we've searched the bloody school for you,' Fee starts.

I look at my book, suddenly remembering what the hell I'm supposed to be doing.

'Tell her,' Kar interrupts.

'It's bloody well two o' clock; the exam's about to start,' Fee snaps at her. 'We'll talk later.'

'Ohmygod. ohmygod, ohmygod,' I say, ignoring them, 'I can't believe I've fallen asleep again, what the hell is wrong with me?'

'It'll be too late later,' Kar interrupts, staring at Fee.

'No, it won't. Flick, the exam is starting, like, *now*, so get your ass in gear and come on.'

I reluctantly stand and throw my books in my bag. 'Guys, I'm screwed, I really am, what the hell am I going to do?'

'Oh for God's sake,' Fee says, dragging me behind her, 'it's common sense, just write down anything.'

'Easy for you to say,' I reply. Sure enough, the corridor is empty when we get downstairs.

'Damn it,' Fee says as we reach the door. Kar pulls it open then turns to say something; instead she stops and gives me this odd look.

'What?' I ask

'Kar, move it,' Fee insists, giving her a push inside.

The exam isn't quite as bad as I'd expected but I still run out of things to write twenty minutes before the end of it. I clear my desk and head straight to the locker room.

I stop. My stomach retches. My knees feel weak. 'Oh my God,' I whisper as I stare at the word LEZZER written in black permanent marker across my locker door. Lesbo, dyke, homo and queer are written all around it. I stand, stunned, just staring at it for ages as my head spins. I want to vomit. The minute I hear the footsteps behind me, I panic. I wonder where the hell I can hide and quickly veer towards the loo but the strap of my bag catches in the door handle and with a loud rip everything falls to the floor.

'Damn it,' I hiss as I quickly bend to pick them up. I'm frantically throwing everything back in when a shadow falls over me. I bite my lip and slowly look up as the first tears sting my eyes.

'Flick, it's OK. Come on, get up,' Kar says, rushing over to me. I shake my head and start to cry, not knowing where to begin or how to explain.

'Flick, the exam's nearly over; they'll be here in a few minutes. Come on, let's go,' she orders.

She pulls me up, grabs my hand and drags me out into the sunlight. Behind us I hear laughing and hollering.

'We'll head home the back way, by the old library,' she says, pulling me along.

Finally, as we turn onto a narrow side road, she slows

down. I walk beside her wishing I were dead. If only I could get home, I think, just close the door on Kar and everyone, I'd never have to face any of this ever again. I know this time I wouldn't fail. Just stay calm, I think, pretend it's all OK, just a few minutes more and she'll be gone and then I can get everything sorted.

Kar sticks her hand into her bag and pulls out a box of ciggies. She lights one and hands it to me. I take a long, slow drag just as her phone beeps. 'Fee's going to meet us at my house,' she says.

'I can't; I have to get home,' I say.

'Why?' she asks. 'Aren't your parents at work?'

'Mam's home early today; we've friends coming. I promised I'd help,' I lie.

She shrugs and we walk in silence for a few minutes.

'So, there was this rumour this morning when we came into school,' she begins as I hand her back the cigarette. She shakes her head and pulls another one from the box, then lights it. 'Danny Brown saw you and Joey leaving the concert on Friday night. He lives on her road. He says everyone knows she's a lezzer.'

I take another drag of the cigarette. 'But I explained that she was my cousin,' I begin.

'Seemingly he asked his Dad,' Kar says before taking another puff. 'You know he's that big solicitor guy that knows nearly everyone in town?'

I don't respond.

'Anyway, he says her parents are foreign and there's no way that ye can be related.'

I secretly curse Danny bloody Brown and his know-it-all Dad. We walk on in silence.

'Your Mam's car isn't there,' Kar says as we reach the house.

'She's probably at the shops,' I say, 'I'll just go in and tidy up till she comes back.'

'Your house is always tidy,' she says; 'your Mam always has it perfect. There's nothing to tidy.'

'I'm just not in the mood.'

But Kar's adamant. 'You're coming to mine and that's it,' she insists.

'Please Kar,' I whisper, 'I can't.'

'I'm not leaving you alone,' she says, grabbing my wrist. I start to cry again when I realise my plan isn't going to work; not here, not now, anyway.

'Kar, I just want to be by myself,' I say. She ignores me and just drags me along. I try to pull my hand away as we head into the estate. 'Kar,' I say through clenched teeth, 'you're bloody well hurting me, let go.'

But she grips my wrist tighter and ignores my complaints.

Once we're in the estate I shut up; the last thing I want to do is to draw attention to myself. I walk wordlessly beside her, my eyes darting back and forth searching for people that aren't there.

'Is that you, love?' Kar's Mam asks the minute she opens the door.

'Yeah, Mam. Flick's with me; we're going upstairs,' she shouts.

By the time we get to the room I've got it all figured out, I'm gonna tell them that Joey is a lezzer but that we're just friends and how a few of us from counselling had arranged to go to the concert but at the last minute the others had chickened out and it ended up just being the two of us. Fee is there already, sprawled across the bed and Kar heads straight over to the dressing table and begins pouring cranberry juice into two glasses. They both look at me and I give a nervous smile and am just about to blurt out my spiel when Kar turns towards me.

'Close the door,' she says as she hands me a glass.

'To finishing exams,' Fee says.

I take a swig. 'Jeez, Kar this is lethal,' I splutter.

'Don't bloody waste it,' she says as I wipe it off my mouth and clothes. 'You hardly thought it was just juice, did you?' she says as she takes a drink.

'To summer holidays and doing absolutely nothing for weeks and weeks and weeks,' Fee interrupts.

'She got a little head start,' Kar says, nodding towards Fee. I take another mouthful and sit on the floor. OK, I'll drink this, I decide, for some Dutch courage then I'll tell them and I'll be home in half an hour. The vodka and cranberry tastes lovely and all too soon it's finished. Kar immediately comes with more.

'Kar, I'll be plastered.'

She brushes it off as she fills my glass. 'Life's too short to worry about crap like that.'

'To boyfriends and late nights and –' Fee sings

'We don't want to know,' Kar butts in. Mam rings at some stage and I explain that I'm with Kar and Fee. Amazingly she doesn't give out, just warns me to be home before ten. Kar has filled up my glass again by the time I'm off the phone.

'Kar, stop! I'll be locked!'

'They won't even smell it off you,' she says as she tips more vodka in.

'I'm sure they'll suss there's something wrong if I can't even stand straight.'

They laugh and Kar runs down for some soakage. So we munch and drink and talk about everything except what's happened at school and for a little while I even stop obsessing about my life being ruined.

'So, are you OK, anyway?' Kar asks out of nowhere. I'm caught totally got off guard so I just shrug and try desperately to remember what I had planned to say.

'The lads are just rotten,' Fee joins in. 'Such imbeciles.' I nod.

'So, do you want to tell us the story?' Kar asks quietly.

I bite my lip, wondering what the hell to say.

'You know my cousin, Sophie? She's a lezzer,' Kar says. 'It's not like it's such a big deal or anything.'

Ohmygod, ohmygod, just please shut up, my mind screams.

'No way,' Fee slurs, 'Sophie's a lezzer? I can't believe it. When the hell did that happen?'

I see Kar giving her the eye to shut up.

'Oh yeah, now I remember,' Fee mumbles.

Kar looks back towards me.

'It really isn't a biggie,' she repeats. 'I've kissed girls before, too.'

'What?' Fee screeches. 'When?'

'Jeez, will you relax, Fee? What the hell is wrong with you?' Kar barks.

I give a little smile but don't take my eyes off Kar.

'Anyway, the last time was at Christmas,' Kar says.

'Ah, everyone kisses at Christmas,' Fee says, brushing her off.

'She was Jake's cousin from America,' Kar says, ignoring her. 'We went out to have a fag and it just happened.'

'Oh my God,' Fee says, 'that's the night we were looking for you for ages!'

Kar lights up. 'Sorry. I was having fun; I guess I didn't notice the time! Anyway, loads of people do it. And the lads, well, they're just jealous that someone as good-looking as you isn't interested in them.'

'They're jealous, for sure,' Fee agrees enthusiastically.

They both look towards me and I dip my head, unable to meet their gaze.

'So ... are ye going out together?' Kar asks tentatively.

I know I could lie and swear that Joey and I are just friends and then sneak around, like for ever ... or just admit to it all; it's not like they don't already think it.

I give a little shrug. 'I guess.'

'Wow,' Fee says.

Kar just sits staring at me.

Almost immediately I'm wishing I hadn't said anything.

'I have to go,' I begin, the tears starting to well up. I stand quickly and put my glass on the dresser.

'Oh, no, you don't,' Kar says, jumping up and running towards me. I barely get time to scream before she grabs me, whirls me round and throws me onto the bed. I barely miss Fee's head. Fee screams as Kar dives on top of me and pins me down.

'Kar,' I shout, squirming under her grip, 'let me go.'

'Quickly, Fee, grab her feet before she gets away,' Kar orders. Fee quickly obeys and plonks herself on my legs.

'Help!' I scream, 'I'm suffocating!'

'If she was on your face you'd be suffocating.' Kar laughs.

There's a knock on the door.

'Karen, is everything OK?' her mother asks timidly. 'I thought I heard a scream.'

'No, we're just chatting!'

We wait until we hear her walking back down the hall before we all burst out laughing. In the excitement Kar has relaxed her grip and Fee has fallen off the bed. I sit up, still laughing.

'Come on, Flick,' Kar says, 'lighten up. Tell us how the hell you met and all the gory details – you know if it was me I would.' She rolls off the bed, finds the end of the vodka and shares it out between us.

'That's not fair,' Fee grumbles, 'you gave me the least.'

'That's because you're already drunk,' Kar says. 'And Flick had a traumatic day; she needs it more. You see,' she says to me, 'there *are* perks to being a lezzer.'

'You did this on purpose,' I say accusingly. 'You planned to get me drunk so I'd talk!'

'Would you have told us otherwise?' she asks. 'We're your friends, Flick, and have been, like, for ever, you're supposed to tell us everything.'

I raise an eyebrow.

'Well, nearly everything,' she corrects herself with a smile. 'So, is telling us this such a bad thing?'

'I suppose not,' I agree reluctantly. I drink most of the glass of vodka before telling them the whole story of Joey and me. The relief is unbelievable.

'What's it like to kiss a girl?' Fee asks, crinkling up her nose.

'It's softer and sweeter than a guy,' I begin.

'And no stubble,' Kar adds.

They ask me a million questions and we end up lying on the bed, chatting and laughing about it for ages. Kar's Mam comes up sometime after eleven to say Dad's at the door. He has to wait there at least ten minutes while Fee and I try and make ourselves look sober and respectable. By half past I've fallen into bed; within seconds I'm asleep.

CHAPTER 55

It's the middle of August and although the holidays are nearly over, they've been the best ever. I went to the new counsellor for a few weeks but because I was in such good form all the time and didn't seem to have any problems or issues she told Mam that she didn't think I needed any more sessions. I can ring at any time if I need to return but for now, I'm free. Yippee!

Better still, I'm madly in love with Joey! Walter's has become our new local haunt; we practically live there. It's this really cool, trendy café on the other side of town that no one I know goes to. Joey doesn't seem to mind but Kar is so unimpressed and keeps telling me avoidance is not a good thing and that I need to confront my fears. Last week she broke up with Arnie and cornered me again.

'It's not fair,' she complained, 'you and Fee are madly in love and have totally forgotten about me.'

'That's not true,' I reply adamantly.

'It is and you know it.'

I'm about to contradict her when she butts in:

'When was the last time we were out together?' she asks.

'Two days ago,' I reply.

'Going to Walter's during the day with you and your girlfriend doesn't count,' she says. 'I mean *out* out! You never come to the park or to the Cove any more,' she says.

'I don't want to go there.'

'You can't give your whole life up, Flick, just cause some guys slag you off,' she says.

'I know, I know,' I say, brushing her off; I've heard this too many times before.

'It's your birthday next week and we're going out!' she suddenly announces.

'OK, but Joey will be away and I was going to wait and have something when she gets back.'

'You can do that, too; we'll have two celebrations,' she says.

I make a face.

'Great,' she says, ignoring me, 'sorted!'

CHAPTER 56

A week later I'm all dressed up and dreading it. I've thought about pretending to be sick so many times but I know that Kar will actually come and drag me out if I do. I hear the doorbell as I fix my hair for the umpteenth time. Within seconds Fee's in my room.

'You look fab. Are you ready?'

'I really don't want to go,' I admit.

'Come on,' she says, grabbing my hand, 'it'll be OK'

The minute we head into the estate a few of the fourth years from school see us and start shouting 'lezzers' at us. Fee gives them the finger but I just keep my head down and walk faster.

Ohmygod, I think, this is going to be the worst night of my life; I just know it. I'm so relieved when we reach Kar's door – that is, of course, until Ryan opens it.

'Hey,' Fee says as she breezes in past him towards the kitchen.

'Hi,' I say coyly, following her.

'Hey,' he says, 'how are you?'

'OK.' I turn bright red. I wonder if he knows about me.

'How were the exams?' he asks.

'Lousy,' I reply, 'and worse has yet to come.'

'Worse?' he asks.

'The results,' I explain. 'Mam and Dad will probably freak when the envelope arrives next week.'

'It's only fifth year,' he shrugs. 'Just don't fail next year or you'll never leave this dump of a town.' I give a quick smile, knowing he's right. 'How were yours?' I ask

'Rough,' he replies, 'I'll have to repeat a few.'

'Oh,' I say, as Kar calls me, 'well, good luck with them. Um, I better go.' I head for the kitchen with Ryan following close behind.

'SURPRISE!'

The shout is deafening. I don't know whether to laugh or cry when I see the rest of the girls in front of me.

'Happy Birthday,' Ryan whispers before they surround me.

I don't get a chance to reply.

'Ohmygod … Ohmygod!' I laugh as they bombard me with gifts. Finally Kar squeezes her way through.

'Wow, you look amazing,' I say when I see her. Almost immediately I turn bright red.

'You never said that to me,' Fee grins from beside me.

'You do, too,' I say, embarrassed.

'Or me,' Katie smirks, giving me a nudge.

'You too.'

'Here, have a drink,' Kar says, 'before you put your foot in it again.'

We all laugh.

'Bottoms up!' Fee smirks as we clink glasses.

I drink half of it before taking a break, knowing that the only way to survive the night is to get totally sozzled. But after just one, the girls are ready to move on.

'Can't we stay here longer?' I plead.

'No way.' Kar is grabbing my hand and dragging me towards the door.

'Please,' I beg.

She turns and looks at me. 'Trust me, it'll be OK'.

The lads are gone when we head back outside. They're probably waiting for us down at the park, I think warily. But instead of crossing the road to the park we head left, then left again.

'Where are we going?' I ask.

'Wait and see,' Fee says as she hands me a Coke bottle from her bag. I take it, hoping her concoction will wash away some of the fear in the pit of my belly.

'So does Ryan know about me?' I ask Kar after a bit.

'Yep,' she says. 'So, does my hair look OK?'

'Yeah it looks great; don't touch it. What did he say?' I ask.

'He said if you gave him a chance he'd be able to change your mind.'

'He did not!'

'Did so. Cross my heart and hope to die,' she says and we both laugh.

I take another swig. He still likes me, I think, smiling to myself. We round another corner and I stop when I see the big ferris wheel in front of me.

'You've got to be kidding,' I say.

'We're going to the carnival!' Fee shrieks. 'It's gonna be great!'

'No way; everyone's going to be there.'

'Yes way,' Kar insists as she drags me along.

'This is the last night and it's going to be fab,' Fee says.

'Please, guys; I can't,' I plead.

'You can,' Kar replies stubbornly. 'You have to do it sooner or later; might as well do it now.'

'Tonight? On my seventeenth birthday? Gee, thanks, guys; you're so thoughtful, such great friends,' I say.

'If it's bad we'll leave straight away,' Kar promises.

I'm bricking it by the time we reach the carnival grounds. The place is mobbed and the noise is deafening. Sue and Kar drag me onto the wheel of death and for a few minutes as my stomach somersaults and my head spins, I forget about everything and just squeal until we stop. Then there's the rollercoaster and waltzers. We're standing contemplating whether to go on them again when a bunch of the lads stroll towards us. I dip my head straight away but not before I see them nudging one another and grinning.

'Oh look, lads,' Tom says, 'the lezzer's back.' They all laugh and I feel myself burning up.

'Shut up, Tom,' Fee shouts.

'We thought we were well and truly rid of her,' Jay says, 'off with those other sicko lezzers.'

'Go to hell, guys,' Katie says.

'On your bike, ya dyke!' Trev says as they all roar laughing again.

For what seems like for ever they throw insults at me and the girls throw them back. I feel sick and ashamed and my head's pounding and all I want to do is run away. I look towards them and suddenly realise that I'm going to be their entertainment for the night; they don't need a carnival with a freak like me around.

As I stand there listening to the abuse, the crowd grows – guys and girls from school attracted by the shouts and laughing. During it all, Kar has stood quietly by me but has never uttered a word – Kar who promised everything would be OK, who told me we'd get out of here if things got too bad. And then in all the turmoil I hear her voice.

'Just go with me, Flick, OK?'

I wonder if we're about to make a run for it but she has this glint in her eye and a smile on her face and suddenly she's pushing me against the wooden rails of the waltzers and she's bending towards me and her lips are on mine and we're kissing. For a second my eyes flick towards her but close again almost immediately. She tastes of candy floss and toffee and she's irresistible. I don't know whether it's because the kiss is so amazing or whether people are stunned into silence but suddenly everything goes so quiet.

Please forgive me, Joey, I think, I know you'll understand when – *if* I tell you. This is Kar just being a great friend and putting herself on the line for me. She was never going to let me run away. Then I stop thinking about everything cause Kar is gently pulling me closer and she tastes so sweet and all I want to do is melt.

A huge cheer goes up; the girls start screaming and shouting and laughing and I can't help but laugh too. Kar pulls away slightly and looks at me with that same grin on her face and I can't make out whether this is all a joke or not.

'Our first kiss,' she whispers. 'How was it?'

'Perfect,' I say with a smile.

'You're all just a bunch of lezzers,' Tom shouts as he and the lads stare at us.

'Would you blame us with talent like you around the place?' Kar asks.

He sticks up his finger as he and the lads turn away in disgust but we all just laugh again.

'We've a long night ahead of us and a carnival to enjoy,' Kar shouts, grabbing my hand.

We start to run back towards the ferris wheel, the

others following, screaming as they go. Kar squeezes my hand a little tighter and I look towards her laughing face.

'Here come the girls!' we roar as we race into the wind, leaving everyone else behind us.